David Jessop was born in Mansfield, England and studied Modern History at Queen Mary College, University of London. He also has a doctorate in History from Dalhousie University, Canada. Most of his life was spent in Finance and Charity work in the UK and North America. *Abchurch Militant* is David's second novel.

For my granddaughter, Cecily, and grandsons, Timothy, Douglas and Christopher. And for friends, Kenneth Pang and W K Law.

David Jessop

ABCHURCH MILITANT

AUSTIN MACAULEY PUBLISHERS

LONDON • CAMBRIDGE • NEW YORK • SHARJAH

A CIP catalogue record for this title is available from the British Library.

ISBN 9781035862856 (Paperback)
ISBN 9781035862863 (Hardback)
ISBN 9781035862870 (ePub e-book)

www.austinmacauley.com

First Published 2024
Austin Macauley Publishers Ltd®
1 Canada Square
Canary Wharf
London
E14 5AA

Chapter 1
The New Bishop

The new Bishop of London, Leo Ezra Normanton, tried but failed to hide his excitement at the announcement in the *Times* newspaper of his appointment to office. He read and reread the piece many times that Monday morning. He had assumed that such an ecclesiastical elevation would happen at some stage of course and over many years had tirelessly made himself suitable, got himself noticed, the obvious candidate for promotion, politically and socially safe. He had ensured that he ticked all the right boxes as modern marketing terminology will indelicately claim. He did have some advantages of course.

His parents with foresight had prepared him for a role in authority by boarding him at a prominent and expensive public school. From there, he had read History at Cambridge and later Theology at Oxford and, although these endeavours had produced only indifferent academic success, he had quickly understood that later in life no one ever enquired concerning the actual quality of your degree. Attendance at Oxford or Cambridge Universities was all that mattered. Afterwards, he had written a few pamphlets and articles on the difficulties and intricacies of Christian belief which fashionably doubted whether there should actually be such a concept as faith or God or even religion itself in the twenty-first century. He publicly eschewed Thomas Cranmer's traditional prayer book describing it as an irrelevance to modern life, and instead happily and unquestioningly used any current popular form of words for all his church services.

His uncle had introduced him to membership of the Athenaeum Club on Pall Mall in London, the place in which to meet those clerics who were very senior in the Church of England. And later, after a little nudging from within the Archbishop of Canterbury's office, although a loner and someone who was only really relaxed in male company, he had finally got married, and he and his wife, a quiet, unobtrusive domestic woman, spent all their summer holidays on the mainland of Europe mixing with continental divines after examining local churches and museums. He had worked very hard indeed to authenticate himself both with relevant authority and also, as he saw it, with the spirit of the age. And, at last, he was being rewarded. It had all been worthwhile.

Now, he was a bishop authenticated by the *Times*, and truth to tell, he was a very senior bishop, and he was barely 50. And he knew that Buckingham Palace must have agreed to the appointment. But the best news of all was that as a senior bishop, he could take his place immediately by right as a member of the House of Lords, the finest London club of them all or so he had often been assured. He smiled to himself and cut out the announcement from the newspaper which he folded up neatly into his wallet. Later, he would ask his wife, Dorothy, to fix it into his personal scrapbook, a job, he knew, she enjoyed doing.

On the Monday morning of this notification in the newspaper and on returning from yet another holiday in Rome, Bishop Leo decided to visit his new office near St Paul's Cathedral. There he intended to meet the staff and get a general feel for the working environment. So he duly arrived, greeted those present, drank coffee and chatted pleasantly with many of them.

He explained that everyone could speak informally to him, and he wanted to be involved with as much of their day-to-day work as possible and expected personally to take all major decisions. Here was a bishop who thought and acted for himself without the need for committees and panels of experts. He would flatten the office chain of command or so he claimed in his enthusiasm on that Monday morning.

Two young clerics, Rev John and Father Adrian, suitably encouraged by his words, put down their coffee cups and stepped forward. They introduced themselves and explained that they had helped the previous bishop in most of his diocesan work, especially on a recent major Anglican project in the City of London which had examined the future of the whole parish structure itself, and they would be available to provide continuity for Bishop Leo and to help him settle in, should he so wish. The bishop smiled, thanked them but then frowned and hesitated. Such a warm offer he knew couldn't easily be refused, especially coming as it did from local diocesan officials when other office staff were watching. But he himself also needed continuity and with that in mind intended to bring with him two senior officials from his previous workplace to help him run his new diocese.

After all, they knew him so well. They always had the answer before he even asked the question. And, in truth, they had linked their careers firmly with his over many years. He just couldn't work without them. He told the office about these colleagues but as he said, he was certain Rev John and Father Adrian would easily fit into an expanding office. There was surely enough work for all in a place like London!

"Well, don't look so worried," the bishop laughed, as the two clerics appeared crestfallen on the news, "I'm sure we will all get along here together as Christ would wish. Now, what's top of the list of priorities at the moment?" He deftly changed the subject on seeing several files thickly stacked by John's desk.

"Well, it's St Mary Abchurch," said John nervously, "one of our worn-out old church buildings off Cannon St. We are about to sign a contract for its sale to a property company. It's a great site and, in the middle of the City of London will provide a large sum for diocesan funds."

"If we are going to have more head office staff here we will need the money," he whispered under his breath to Father Adrian as an aside.

"Sounds straightforward," laughed the new bishop. "Hope all my problems are this easy. Do I need to sign papers for the arrangement of sale or whatever?"

He took out his inscribed fountain pen, a gift from his widowed mother after he had been accepted to study at Cambridge University many years before. "Oh, sorry, another time, now I have to go," he looked at his watch. "The Archbishop of York, an old friend, has agreed to show me around the Lords, the House of Lords you understand," he whispered conspiratorially. "I can't be late." And, with that, he carefully put away his treasured pen, gathered up his papers and without saying goodbye to anyone rushed out to a waiting taxi which had appeared in the yard. His first morning in the office was now complete, and he thought it a great success.

Rev John looked at Father Adrian.

"Well. I'm not sure what to make of that Adrian. He obviously hasn't been briefed about all the trouble we have had with St Mary Abchurch and that old vicar and his snobbish wife who used to be there. Oh, well, the contract is nearly ready for signing. We've done our job," he shrugged his shoulders as he walked over to his desk.

At that moment, a flustered secretary rushed in.

"Oh, John," she exclaimed, "don't sit down yet. A large Pickfords Removals lorry has just driven into the yard. It's scraped the side wall; you probably heard that grinding noise. Apparently, we are taking delivery of two very big mahogany desks, chairs, sofas, charts and several enormous antique wooden cabinets of files and books. Do you know anything about it?"

Rev John groaned and said he couldn't be sure, but he might probably guess what it all meant. "It's the acolytes of the new bishop I suspect," he said bitterly. "The two people we have just been told about who always work with him."

He was right of course and on cue two middle-aged rather corpulent clergymen walked purposefully into the office. "I'm Bryan Peacock," announced the first one by way of introduction. "That's Bryan with a 'y'. You have no idea how it annoys me when my name is misspelt. I'm only saying this once. Please make sure all the secretaries are informed. Always a 'y' never an 'i'," he intoned.

Then peering around the office, he continued, "Now, we are taking delivery of several files and large pieces of furniture, so let me look at your accommodation here." And, with that, he walked into one of the adjoining meeting rooms.

"I think Jude and I will put our material into this first conference room. It is commodious enough for our antique mahogany desks, chairs and sofas. and I like the high ceiling.

"It suggests ancient authority as well as a modern business structure. Well, that's settled. Now, for proper greetings. You two must be John and Adrian. The bishop warned us there would be 'inherited staff'. Sorry, my little joke," he smirked. "Good to meet you." He offered and quickly withdrew a moist warm hand.

"Now," he continued, "I think the four of us should get together so that I can outline how the office will be run under the new regime and more broadly what Bishop Leo will expect from us all going forward. You've now met your new bishop I understand. Well, I've known the dear man for many years. I was at Cambridge with him. I used to read his essays before he handed them in and sometimes edited or actually rewrote them, but let that be our little secret," he tapped his nose.

"As you will find out, he is very easy-going except over the issue of church services. He hates old-fashioned expressions and formularies, particularly Cranmer's Book of Common Prayer. He describes churches which use the old prayer book as CO places. That's his shorthand for 'Cranmer Obsessed'. When he finishes his work in this diocese no one who wants a serious career in the church will be using it.

"The other thing to tell you is that he is very rigid in his working practices. That's why he likes to deal through me. After several years, I obviously understand how he works, what he expects and how he operates in the office environment. So I will run the day-to-day church proceedings and will be the conduit from the general office to the bishop."

Each of the four clerics had by now moved to the adjoining meeting room, the one which would apparently become an office. Adrian was still drinking coffee and listening, but John feeling himself becoming more and more agitated and getting very red in the face decided it was time to break his silence.

"Just a minute," he said. "I appreciate that you two have been with the bishop for a very long time, even as far back as a university, but Adrian and I know this particular diocese very well. We are versed in its peculiarities and have spent most of our careers here. And not half an hour ago we heard the new bishop say that he liked an informal, flat office structure, his door was always open, and we could pop in anytime to discuss issues. He didn't mention an office hierarchy."

"Yes," laughed Bryan, "we have heard that speech often in the past. The theory is good and Bishop Leo has been on quite a few management courses at some of the best business schools, but in reality, he can only work in a strictly structured atmosphere. The truth is he expects me to run the place. It gives him inner peace he says. So please do come through me if you need contact with Bishop Leo. Better that we sort out this organisational matter from the start.

"No need for us to fall out over it. As the bishop often says, Christ would expect us all to work together. A smoothly running diocesan office is the key to a successful bishopric. As I'm sure, you would both agree."

He turned to Jude who like Adrian had been silent all this time. "Fancy a very early lunch, Jude? I walked around the local streets last month just to become familiar with the area, and I noticed there's a lovely little French bistro nearby which would suit us both. We could share a carafe of red wine, even though it's probably a bit of an indulgence on a Monday morning. It would clear our minds for the tasks ahead. There is obviously so much to be done and sorted out in the Diocese of London."

The two colleagues breezed out of the office leaving Rev John and Father Adrian standing alone.

Watching them leave, Rev John was clearly still very upset. He himself had been given some authority in the church at an early age, so he had naturally become used to giving rather than obeying commands.

"I shall ask for a transfer to another diocese," he said precipitously to Father Adrian as he tried to avoid the removal men who were now noisily shifting desks and cabinets through the office.

"Now, don't be silly," Adrian counselled him calmly. "Don't play their game. The London diocese is our territory. We know the people, the churches and the issues. We are on familiar terms with dozens of priests in the area in a way these newcomers can never match.

"Just let them get used to the place. They will settle down. Jude seems a nice friendly chap, at least he smiles a lot even if he doesn't say much. Come on let's have our own early lunch and talk matters through. Bishop Leo after all is like us in one respect, he is not a Book of Common Prayer minister.

"Yes, you are right," sighed John. "I can overreact. Come on let's leave this noise and bustle, a chat over a pub lunch would be good." The two colleagues walked out into the busy street in front of the cathedral, down Ludgate Hill towards their favourite tavern near the church of St Martin.

Meanwhile, having left the diocesan office, Bishop Leo had made his way by taxi to the House of Lords, where the Archbishop of York was already waiting for him. They warmly shook hands and for the next hour spent time walking around the empty debating chamber and the various committee rooms. Leo was introduced to other bishops and various lords from all political parties and factions of the House. The Archbishop was a good guide and by early afternoon Leo was starting to relax and feel very much at home.

"How much time can I expect to spend in the chamber of the House of Lords?" he asked the Archbishop.

"Well, that's very much up to you," replied the Archbishop. "In the Church of England, we do, of course, have a rota of times and bishops to make sure that all debates are covered. The constitution of the country demands that the church is always present. So there will be certain days that you will be expected to be here. But in addition to that, of course, you can be here as much as your diocesan duties will allow.

"You are a senior bishop, so please try and speak in the chamber when you have settled in. The Archbishop of Canterbury will notice who speaks in debate, as well as the subject of that discussion of course. His assistants keep him very much up to date on all such matters. My advice would be to spend as much time here as you possibly can. This is where the power is."

And he winked knowingly at Bishop Leo. "Oh, by the way, I should mention that Canterbury often takes trusted bishops with him on his many overseas trips. Sitting with the Archbishop on a long aeroplane flight is an excellent way to learn about the church at top levels and obviously get noticed. People who travel with Canterbury also get regularly consulted and generally listened to."

"Now, as this is your first time, here I think I can treat you to a rather tasty late lunch," he continued. "As I hope you will see, the meals in the House of Lords are really first class, better than most restaurants outside in Westminster, and the wine list is quite extensive. If they don't have a wine you like, just tell the waiter, and he will certainly have it next time you dine here. Believe me, you won't be disappointed."

Bishop Leo smiled in return, involuntarily rubbed his hands and straightened his clerical collar. The first day at work in his new post had gone rather well he thought. The staff seemed knowledgeable and importantly, he convinced himself, Bryan and Jude would fit easily into his new office. He knew he had been right to bring them along with him.

He sensed he was going to enjoy being the Bishop of London and bringing the diocese up to date with ecclesiastical fashions. He smiled to himself and finished his Lobster Thermidor. When he got home later he must remember to ask Dorothy to fix the *Times* announcement into his career scrapbook.

Chapter 2
Project WrenFuture

During the following week, Rev John, assisted occasionally by Father Adrian, completed the final parts of the contract to sell St Mary Abchurch. Project WrenFuture they had named it. Both men had spent many months drawing up the proposals and had put together a shortlist of potential property developers who could knock down the church and replace it with a modern office development. Just before Bishop Leo had been confirmed in office a final company, Thoughtful Properties Ltd, a well-known building group, had been announced as the chosen bidder.

TPL as they liked to be called had submitted its plans which were not only cost-effective for its shareholders but also importantly included ideas which would link the old St Mary Abchurch to the new small tower they intended to build in its place. In addition, the Church of England would keep a small financial interest in the new development, a detail which was important for TPL as it might encourage the Anglican Church to transact more such deals with the property group in the future.

This concept of joint development had also been very important for the previous bishop. The diocese was keen not to be seen merely as dumping an old building but rather as maintaining a role in the area which replaced it. TPL's scheme was certainly revolutionary, or so it appeared to both the church and the company's board because it proposed taking some of the features out of St Mary Abchurch and incorporating them within the new tower. This was also a notion which had inspired the former bishop and helped ensure that TPL finally beat the competition. Now, it was being left to Bishop Leo to sign the contract of sale and explain the finer points to the press.

"I will chat to Bishop Leo to ensure he understands all the details that we have worked out over the past months. Parts of this arrangement and our ongoing financial relationship with TPL are somewhat complex and in fact quite original especially those incorporating parts of the old church into the new structure," John explained to Bryan. "Bishop Leo might inevitably come to see this sale as defining his tenure of office here. I'm not exaggerating.

"It is that important. He really does need to be aware of the pressure points of the deal, I think that's the usual jargon, as in this case, I'm sure the newspapers and television will inevitably take a big interest now that we are proposing to sell a church designed by Sir Christopher Wren. He was after all a rather famous English architect."

"Yes, I know who Sir Christopher Wren was," said Bryan loudly and sarcastically, "but there is no need for you to see Leo." Bryan took charge firmly. "Over the past few days, I have got an understanding of how this diocese operates. I will take the contract to the bishop. Just give me the outlines of the proposal.

"It can't be that complicated, putting up an office block. The City of London is full of such new buildings. The important details are to explain exactly what we intend to do with the money and to assure the Archbishop of Canterbury's office that we did get the best price for the land. I assume you both addressed important issues like that when you put the deal together. I hope you haven't just given away a valuable asset.

"I remember when Leo was an archdeacon in the Midlands one of his rural deans had no real understanding of the value of the church land he was selling. I had to reopen the whole negotiation. It added months to the project. But as it turned out the diocese was very pleased that I had done so. Through my dedicated efforts, the church's remuneration increased significantly." Bryan beamed.

"The bishop leaves for the House of Lords in ten minutes," a secretary interrupted.

John shrugged his shoulders, gave the agreement and a few notes to Bryan and returned to his desk. "Well, it's all there: Prices, bidders, reason for sale, church history, our future financial understanding with TPL, other issues involved, the lot." He grimaced towards Father Adrian and sat down.

Bryan quickly perused the contract and John's notes and disappeared into the bishop's office where he found Leo pacing up and down in something of a fluster.

"Do please be quick, Bryan. I'm off to the Lords in a few minutes, and I expect to be called upon to speak in the debate on the provision of free deckchairs at seaside towns," said Bishop Leo impatiently. "I practised giving a speech at home in front of the bathroom mirror this morning but actually being there and talking in the Lords is quite a different proposition as I'm sure you can understand."

"Well," said Bryan, "putting it briefly and quickly, as you know, Rev John and Father Adrian have, after endless months I might add, finally drawn up a contract to sell one of our many churches. A bit of a no-brainer really, goodness only knows why they had to work for so long on the deal. Have you seen just how many churches we have around here, far too many to be religiously healthy in such a small area. Even I get the names confused, and I've been a priest as you know for years. You turn a corner, and there is yet another church."

"Yes, yes, please do continue, Bryan," said the bishop impatiently, "I really am in a hurry."

Looking down at the contract and John's notes, Bryan continued, "Well, we are apparently selling a church called St Mary Abchurch to Thoughtful Properties Ltd, TPL. I suspect you might have met some of the board already perhaps. Some are well-known national figures."

"Yes, of course, I have," beamed Leo. "The chairman is in the House of Lords. The Archbishop of York introduced me to him on my first morning. A lovely man. I might be able to go over the final details with him over dinner there.

"I hope nothing is contentious in the contract. I wouldn't want to upset TPL at this stage. I believe the chairman and his wife even live near me in Richmond-on-Thames, he added as an afterthought."

"No, nothing controversial, I don't think so," said Bryan, cautiously examining John's notes again. "Apparently, TPL wants to build two models of the area and perhaps hold a small public meeting to ensure the sale gets full transparency, and they are keen for the diocese to be involved in all this because of our continuing relationship, albeit a small token one, with ownership of the project.

"Yes, good idea. But do make sure you and Jude have walked around the building before I actually approve anything. That is very important. I rely on you both totally. I shall need to see over it as well of course if my busy schedule allows.

"Now, I'm sorry to hurry you Bryan, but I really must get to my car. I think the chauffeur is there already. Talk to me tomorrow if anything is worrying you."

The bishop grabbed his leather briefcase and rushed out to the yard where the car was already warmed up and waiting.

Bryan returned, ignored Rev John and dropped the contract onto Jude's desk.

"Well, what did the bishop say?" Jude asked.

"Not a lot. He's in a panic about some debate in the Lords. As to St Mary Abchurch, I got the impression that he doesn't seem to think anyone will be bothered much about the sale. He was quite relaxed. He knows the chairman of TPL, at least they both sit in the Lords apparently," said Bryan. "He wants us to look over the building as soon as possible, so we can answer any final questions he might have. In fact, thinking about it; do you fancy a stroll over there now while the project is fresh in my mind?"

"Yes, excellent idea," agreed Jude and the two colleagues strode out into the midday sunshine.

Unfortunately, neither Bryan nor Jude was familiar with London. In fact, both men nursed an inner distaste for what they imagined to be the cultural superiority of the place. Their careers to date unusually had barely touched the capital, and their knowledge of the Square Mile, the City of London, in particular, was very scant indeed. And, of course, neither man had bothered to consult with Rev John or Father Adrian or any other local staff to ask for directions. Once outside the office and having walked in front of St Paul's Cathedral, they turned the corner of the building, past the underground tube station and eventually down the main thoroughfare in front of them, called Cheapside.

"I think we need to go down one of these alleyways on the right, past this church, St Mary Le Bow," said Bryan, carefully reading the church sign. A little later having meandered past shops, cafes and a hairdresser in Bow Lane they found themselves in front of yet another church, the church of St Mary Aldermary. By now, the streets were filling up with office workers jostling and hurrying to lunch at favourite restaurants and pubs.

"Oh, there's Sweetings over there, the fish restaurant, one of Leo's favourites," said Jude pointing. "I've heard him talking to Dorothy on the phone about Sweetings and the quality of the fresh fish there. I'm sure we must be going in the right direction."

A little further on they walked past the Mansion House and suddenly found themselves in a mass of people being pressed across King William Street towards yet another church, the church of St Mary Woolnoth, very close to the Royal Exchange and the Bank of England.

"See what I mean," snapped Bryan in exasperation. "As I said to Leo, far too many churches. Even as a Christian, I think we can have too many places of worship."

Time by now was getting on and still there was no sign of St Mary Abchurch. They asked directions from a smartly dressed young man, but he turned out to be an overseas tourist who was as lost as they were and had never heard of the church they mentioned.

"I left my phone at the office with its electronic map. All these damn churches are called St Mary," complained Bryan to the crowd in general and a startled old lady in particular. "What sort of imagination calls all the churches in a place St Mary! Yes, don't tell me that medieval Catholic England felt it had a special affinity with the Virgin Mary.

"I know that, but even so, there are dozens of churches named St Mary, or so it seems. The truth is I just don't like London I have to admit it, Jude. And the City of London only feeds my prejudice. There is that smell of historical superiority everywhere."

"Look," said Jude nodding in agreement as he tripped over the kerb, "I'm getting rather hot and bothered, and I need a drink. Pushing into these crowds is giving me a headache. Let's have a glass of wine at a pub and look for St Mary Abchurch another day. We have obviously taken the wrong turn somewhere. The church won't move. We can look again later in the week when we won't be so hurried."

The colleagues turned round and retraced their steps back up Queen Victoria Street, passing the Mansion House and then Sweetings a second time before luckily finding a busy tavern for a brief stop. Later, after a couple of wrong turns took them close to another church, St Vedast, they saw the cathedral nearby and hurried back breathlessly to the diocesan offices.

Rev John and Father Adrian were talking in low whispers as they entered.

Bryan spoke first. "What are you plotting now, you two? Just my little joke. Calm down," he said seeing a look of disgust on Father Adrian's face.

"We were wondering if the bishop had indicated when the contract would be signed," Rev John said diffidently.

"Nothing to get upset about. Bishop Leo will work out the details with the chairman of Thoughtful Properties who apparently is also a member of the House of Lords. See, it often helps to mix in those elevated circles," said Bryan sanctimoniously. "In the meantime, you two can continue your discussions with TPL about some of the finer details of the proposal. I see from the notes I took into Bishop Leo that you, Rev John, will be having a further meeting with them about some of the artefacts they want to incorporate into the new tower."

"Yes, I have a meeting fixed up actually in St Mary Abchurch for later in the week," said John.

"How was St Mary Abchurch? Rumour says it's supposed to be quite beautiful inside with an amazing dome," said Father Adrian. "As yet, we both have only seen it from the street, so you two have one over us there."

"Oh yes, St Mary Abchurch," stammered Bryan pompously flourishing his hand in the air. "Well, it's just a church, an old church like all the rest around here. Nothing that special in spite of all the talk about Christopher Wren. We didn't hang around very long." And, with that, he went back to his mahogany desk and continued his all-consuming study of the senior London clergymen listed in Crockford's Church of England Clerical Directory.

"All very strange," whispered Rev John to Father Adrian. "They can't have been inside either. I've just noticed that the only front door key is still undisturbed at the side of my desk drawer." Both men looked at each other and giggled silently.

"It's a bit unchristian of me to say it," John continued, "but do you notice that Bryan always walks around with a sheet of paper in his hand and a studious expression on his face? I assume it's his way of proving he is actually doing some work. Well, anyway, I'm not fooled."

"Oh, my word just forget him, John! He is taking over your life. Go yourself and look over the church and decide if we are really doing the right thing in selling it," said Father Adrian, "although I guess it's rather late now to be talking like that, the decision has already been taken out of our hands."

Chapter 3
St Mary Abchurch

As arranged, later the same week Rev John met up with Austin and Eric, two senior employees from Thoughtful Properties Ltd, to look inside St Mary Abchurch. They decided to have lunch first at the Vintry public house in Abchurch Yard. The early spring day was sunny and warm so the three sat at a table in the open air in the courtyard in front of the boarded-up church.

After ordering the meal, John spoke first, even surprising himself at his own candour. "To be truthful, I am starting to feel a little nervous about selling this place at all," he pointed to the church, "let alone selling it to a building concern, even one as well-known as yours. I'm not trying to bid up the price," he sighed, "I suppose I've just worked too long on the scheme and now suddenly it's actually here, and we are ready to sign I'm somewhat deflated. And sitting here in the sunshine I can really appreciate, strangely perhaps for the first time, that it's a really old church we are about to destroy."

Austin glanced quickly at Eric, obviously anticipating that the diocesan authorities might become concerned as the day of the proposed sale drew close.

"Rev John," he said, calmly repeating the well-worn arguments voiced recently around the company's board table. "Look at it this way, the diocese and indeed the wider Church of England will not be losing a church, rather they will be selling an underused site which will form part of a vigorous development which is intended to breathe new life into an important area of the City of London. Just look at this dirty old derelict place behind us covered with boards and yellow graffiti, hardly a good advertisement for the Church of England or indeed for the Christian faith generally. And moreover don't forget crucially our concept will have a distinctly religious element. Such an idea, a combination of the church and a property company, is exploratory and new for both parties.

"We are both feeling our way over this deal. That's the key point surely. We are not just building yet another office block which has no connection with the past. As I think our chairman will explain to your Bishop Leo, we want to keep some of the artefacts such as the covered font which I believe you have in the church and the wooden altarpiece, so we can re-erect them inside glass screens within our new foyer, to provide a vivid backdrop when we host an Evensong service which we intend to do at least once and perhaps twice a year in the main entrance of the new block. The previous bishop was very taken with this concept, and I was led to believe that you, Rev John, were enthusiastic about it too.

"We plan to put up beautifully polished wooden signs telling the history of the area and the importance of these treasured artefacts. You in the Anglican Church will benefit twice over. The sale monies will enable the diocese to pursue its Christian mission and St Mary Abchurch won't die but will continue to exist on the same site as always, albeit I realise in a changed form." He looked at Eric for support.

"Yes," agreed Eric, stabbing a fork at his rare steak, "Let's all be honest Rev John. Just look at the place. It's dilapidated, all but derelict. The hoarding is concealing a building way past its time and usefulness. The money needed to modernise it would be an astronomical amount and when you had done the repairs no one would ever go inside anyway.

"Just money, a lot of money which I know the diocese doesn't have, being thrown away. Incidentally, over the past few weeks, I have made it a personal mission to read various guidebooks, and it seems to me that they all concentrate on the items to be found inside anyway, not on the actual building itself, with the possible exception of the dome. So we will be taking away the moveable pieces and saving them not throwing them away. They will remain in the same area of the City of London for which they were made in the first place. So both sides gain from this arrangement, church and company."

"Yes, yes," agreed John wearily, "I realise that. I'm being very silly. I just wanted reassurance. When you are in my position you know, you meet vested interests with powerful friends who can make even the most innocuous concept seem nasty. There are so many societies for this or that historical enterprise, all working as far as I can see to stop any modern development.

"I'm sure five years from now we will all be relieved that the sale went through so efficiently." He poured himself another glass of claret. "Perhaps after we have looked around the church we can go into the finer points of the scheme over your drawings and plans back in my office. You can tell me about some of the neighbouring buildings you are also buying.

"You can then let me have details of the models being made of the refreshed Abchurch Yard, as well as the public presentation you are organising in the city. By the way, rather embarrassingly I have to admit that today is my first visit inside St Mary Abchurch as it is indeed for you two. I've heard about the items you mention of course, but I have never actually seen them. So it's virgin territory for the three of us."

They finished their agreeable meal in the spring sunshine, paid the bill and walked over to look inside the boarded-up church. John, carrying his iPad, produced a set of keys from his pocket and after removing the wooden hoarding he led the way up the few steps and unlocked the main door.

The church they entered that late spring afternoon, St Mary Abchurch, is one of the famous architects, Sir Christopher Wren's, finest masterpieces. Built in the 1680s it is an almost square open space, all the usual deference to medieval aisles between gothic pillars swept away. The church supports a massive dome on its walls. Plain not stained glass windows let in as much as possible of God's pure light, itself very much a revolutionary concept in the seventeenth century. In such an open, large, barn-like interior, incumbents have nowhere to hide.

They are always on view no matter where they choose to sit, kneel or stand during Divine Service. Here they are part of the congregation not cut off from and superior to it as they sometimes seem to be in other churches. Many previous vicars and curates had responded well to this design and had often spoken about the warm Christian ambience which oozes from it because of its shape and the wooden decorations of its space. The dome, painted to show Christ's angels in paradise, appears to envelop and protect the whole congregation with a heavenly ceiling, a representation, for those looking upwards, of the final reward for all God-fearing children. And the building of course houses many old artefacts, the items which John had come to discover for himself today.

"I will fasten us in if you don't mind," John said. "It's amazing to me but as soon as we open the door here we get people wanting to look around. I really wonder why they don't have better things to do. You wouldn't believe the number of people who write to or email the bishop asking for permission to see the place. Luckily he just refuses all requests and says the building is dangerous."

"Is it dangerous?" asked Eric, suddenly somewhat alarmed.

"I've no idea," said Rev John. "It was apparently very busy the other year when we had the previous vicar here, the troublesome one with the snobbish wife I think I may have told you about, and no one ever mentioned danger or Health and Safety laws then. I don't think such an issue was ever brought up."

Once inside St Mary Abchurch, the three started to explore, Eric and Austin produced tape measures to confirm the size of the various fixed wall monuments, while John checked off the ornaments from a list on his iPad. He noted the reredos behind the altar by the famous seventeenth-century carver, Grinling Gibbons, adorned with wooden ribbons of fruit; the panels containing the Ten Commandments, Creed and Lord's Prayer; the four large wooden urns fixed up high; the wooden pulpit; the heavy wooden communion table; the stone font with a polished wooden cover; the royal coat of arms on the west wall; two magnificent sword rests; and two ancient poor boxes. He murmured to himself, "Yes, all is as it should be." The place was very dusty although, except for the dirt, it did seem to be in well-kept order. And it looked rather better inside than it did from the street.

"I think with a quick clean you could actually hold a service here as though St Mary Abchurch had been in continuous use for years," said Eric as if reading John's mind. "It's in much better condition than I ever imagined or was led to believe."

"No more talk like that," whispered Austin shooting a warning glance at Eric.

Then, loudly, "Professionally if asked, I would say it's highly dangerous. Bits of plaster might easily drop off the dome and cause serious damage. And all that wood. Everywhere you look there's wood, wooden pews, an altarpiece, an enormous pulpit, a font cover, poor boxes, tables and chairs. It's all wood, a serious fire trap.

"No signs either, indicating which are the emergency exits. Just not up to the requirements of modern building standards. One careless match falling onto paper would be all that was required to set fire to the lot." He wagged his head sadly.

"And just look at the electrics," he continued. "I imagine that these wires are now very old and frankly dangerous. It's true that the lights do appear to work," he added after flicking a few switches, "but still I'm surprised the fire service didn't condemn the place years ago. It really would be a silly waste of money to try updating this church. I will be very happy to confirm as much to our chairman and your bishop. It would be throwing good money after bad."

When they walked over to the font Austin lifted the heavy wooden cover. "So this is the famous covered font. This will look lovely fastened inside a glass case," he ventured. "It must have suffered terribly over the years being constantly pushed up and down.

"The whole thing now looks very unstable and wobbly. Can you imagine having your baby christened under such a contraption? What if it suddenly fell down? And who exactly are these four wooden figures on top?"

John consulted the list on his iPad. "The four apostles apparently," he said, "Matthew, Mark, Luke and John."

"And the wood behind the altar over there, the reredos or whatever you call it," Austin continued without listening. "I understand from our chairman that it must have been stained dark brown by the Victorians. Well, we would get some of the best wood restorers to put it back to its original lighter colour. We would then use it to line the entrance foyer in our new building. It would form a stunning backdrop to the annual Evensong service that our chairman will speak about to your bishop."

Walking up the aisle, he strained to look upward at the painted dome.

"You know," he ventured, "I really am surprised that a domed roof like that, painted or not, can be allowed even to exist in a building that was ever used by the general public. And to think this place has had services for hundreds of years. The whole building must be a real death trap. As I said before, you can see from here that pieces of masonry have fallen off in the past.

"TPL will take away the best segments of the domed roof and perhaps after making them safe by cutting them up, display them in glass cases in our main lifts. So you see we won't be destroying the existing church. We will be enabling it to come alive again and remain in this area of the City of London. There is so much to do to make St Mary Abchurch breathe anew in the twenty-first century.

"By the way, before I forget, our directors are very anxious to give the lifts in the new building ecclesiastical names to emphasise the Christian heritage of this part of the City of London and to link it to its religious past. We haven't finalised the names yet but perhaps 'matins', 'trinity', 'communion' might be good titles we all thought. My secretary found the words in that prayer book you lent us. She was married in her local village church I believe," he said by way of further explanation.

Approaching the altar, Austin suddenly turned round to face the body of the church. "Now, I don't want to upset you Rev John, but we wouldn't want any of the pews. The board is quite firm on that point," he continued. "I don't know how old they are but perhaps I could suggest that they might be redeployed in another London church or broken up or sold further afield if you don't want to destroy them."

"I don't think we would put them in another church here in the city," interrupted Rev John. "Over the last few years, we have stripped the pews from many churches in the City of London. We have done so almost with a religious zeal. We have freed up the nave for other uses and replaced the benches with stacked chairs instead which are so much more adaptable to modern services. A big open area instead of fixed pews also makes the space attractive for choirs, musical evenings, yoga classes or all types of lectures. I will discuss this further with the bishop but actually giving them away to a poor parish overseas would be my first thought."

Austin nodded his approval. "Pews in churches are such an old-fashioned idea. I'm not religious myself, but I associate wooden pews with stories from my grandma about her local Baptist chapel. In fact, as Eric has often heard me say, knocking down her church and redeveloping the site in Cornwall first got me interested in the building business itself several years ago."

"I don't agree with Austin about religion," Eric later whispered to John. "I always went to church with my parents when I was growing up in Norfolk. Some of my happiest memories come from being in church. I remember once having a pound coin and a twenty-pence piece in my pocket. Dad had given me the twenty-pence piece for the collection and foolishly I put my pound in the collection bag by mistake.

"I just couldn't afford to give a pound as it was my pocket money. I was so worried and nervous about the whole business. Eventually, after the service, I plucked up the courage and went and blurted out my story to the vicar, and he laughed and exchanged the coins for me. Just one of those warm things you remember about the church and your vicar when you are young I suppose."

John understanding smiled. He by now had put away his iPad and was also walking slowly up to the altar starting to sense the spirituality of the place when to his surprise he saw a decayed Christmas poinsettia on a stand at the back of the building, and wedged underneath was protruding a dusty white envelope. He silently retrieved it and found written on the front 'For the next vicar of St Mary Abchurch from Rev

Aubrey Braithwaite'. He said nothing to the others, who were still examining the pews, and hastily slipped the envelope into his pocket.

Eric next climbed the stairs leading to the pulpit. "This wood is still in good condition," he said, "no obvious sign of beetle or damage, although it is too dark and heavy for modern use. I don't think the company will want it. We might unscrew this pulpit door and place it with the font in the glass case in the foyer of the new building would be my first thought, however, if the diocese doesn't need it."

"The guidebooks do enthuse strongly about it," said Rev John, "so if TPL doesn't want it I think we may persuade another church in London to adopt it. But I'm sure you can have the door. We can decide the details later."

"Actually," interrupted Austin, "Eric's mention of the foyer gets me thinking. I see you have a model of a large bird over there, perched over its young."

"Oh, yes, the pelican I think you mean," said John. "Protestant England used to like images of pelicans in the seventeenth century. They are supposed to feed their young with their own blood, a hint of the Communion Service. According to my inventory, this one used to be outside on the roof but nearly came to grief apparently during a major storm in the early 1700s.

"What do you intend to do with it Rev John?" asked Austin. "Because if you don't need it, I'm thinking we could buy it to put over our information desk. A talking point at the new reception."

"I can't see a problem with such an idea," said John. "Consider it as a gift from the diocese to cement our new partnership. I will mention it to the bishop."

"I think that just leaves the main organ," said Oliver. "It looks like a formidable instrument. Obviously, we wouldn't want that. Please let the bishop know. Could you find a ready market for it or would you want us to cart it away?"

"Well, actually, that might be very easily achieved, the ready market I mean," said John. "According to my list, it is an amalgamation of various organ pieces from other instruments rescued from churches bombed in the city in the last war. I'm sure we could distribute pieces around churches in London. Oh, by the way, we have forgotten the church bell hanging in the main tower. The old vicar who used to be here arranged for it to be refurbished—against our advice, I suspect—and apparently, he blessed it one Christmas just before he retired." He thought of the dusty envelope now hidden in his pocket.

"Oh, there must be a ready market for refurbished church bells," said Austin.

"Certainly, the company couldn't use it. Again put it on your list to ask the bishop."

After another tour around the church, the three walked slowly out into the spring sunshine and John searched for his key to lock the door. Eric and Austin were obviously feeling happy with the way the business was progressing and their role in organising it. After all, mused John, the WrenFuture project for them was probably just one of a handful of building schemes they were working on at the moment. A cynic might observe it was merely a single contribution to their no doubt large annual Christmas bonus.

But, for John, in spite of his obvious relief that the contract was almost complete and ready for signing, the sale of the church of St Mary Abchurch could never be just another business deal. He realised that, now he had been inside, seen its beauty and had started to appreciate its history. He had originally been very keen to sell off the church but that afternoon he suddenly started to have more doubts. He became very quiet. He remembered that the building was after all a church, and what was his faith about if not a collection of churches?

And this church in particular he now understood after his tour, was one of the finest examples of Sir Christopher Wren's work. He hadn't fully appreciated that fact in the past. He ought to have called in here when the church was so active. The visit today had interested and impressed him but at the same time deeply troubled him. He knew now that his eyes saw the place completely differently from the eyes of his guests.

He could tell this from the occasional comments made by Austin and Eric. Uncharacteristically therefore he was rather subdued when he came to lock the door. He told himself that he had worked so hard on the sale that inevitably he would now feel a little deflated. His downbeat mood was only to be expected. But really, he knew, it was more than this. As he was leaving the church and the TPL staff were chatting together, he took one last look around the deserted premises, and he felt suddenly as if the generations of the ages were looking down on him, sad and distressed, from their vantage point in the domed ceiling.

Walking over the various ledger stones set in the floor he couldn't help but think of the men, women and children who had moved through life, century after century, on this very spot, guided faithfully by a succession of vicars and curates at St Mary Abchurch. Those very pews which would now be destroyed or sold abroad had been filled with chatter, laughter, sadness, happiness, prayers and singing. The font he knew would have witnessed countless baptisms. By their sermons from the pulpit, vicars would have encouraged and exhorted generations of Christian folk to lead better lives. The local life of the parish had throbbed continuously here year after year, decade after decade, and century following century as the nation's history had played out at first on a national and later on an international stage.

He could sense that just by walking around the building. History was here in St Mary Abchurch for any sensitive individual to see and feel it. The magnificent monument on the east wall, one of those which Eric and Austin had measured so carefully, was itself dedicated to a former Protestant Lord Mayor of London, Patience Ward, who had been compelled to escape to the continent when the church had first opened during the brief reign of King James II. Congregations had been christened, married and buried here to the sound of that bell. The words of the Book of Common Prayer, the prayer book he had ridiculed so often in the past and the book hated by the new bishop had echoed around these premises and had been repeated here many countless thousands of times.

The phrases of the prayer book and the King James Bible would have been known to everyone. Incumbents would have expected their congregations to be well versed in both books, learnt of course originally in Sunday School along with the Catechism and the 39 Articles of Religion. Now, all this would be abandoned and lost and not appreciated or even understood by future generations, and he, John, was not only enabling this destruction but was also driving it forward seemingly enthusiastically and for what, really only for money. The one phrase from the Book of Common Prayer which he did remember 'The Peace of God which passeth all understanding' kept whirling around in his mind as he left the church. How many honest upright Christians had heard numerous vicars say these very words before they themselves departed through these same doors after Divine Service?

As he turned the key in the lock and walked out into the sunshine, he tried to smile and shrug off such thoughts and his downbeat mood.

That envelope hidden under the dead poinsettia has unnerved me, he thought. *Or perhaps I just had too much claret at lunch. My mood will pass. But Cranmer's expression persisted in swirling endlessly round and round in his mind for the rest of the day. 'The Peace of God which passeth all understanding'.*

Out loud and trying to be enthusiastic, he said to Austin and Eric, "Now, let's go down Cannon St to my office near the cathedral and look over your drawings and maps in more detail. I'm particularly interested in how your plans to construct those models of Abchurch Yard are progressing."

Chapter 4
Matters Develop

Over the next few days, to the casual observer, the business of the diocese continued as before. The ripples created by the arrival of a new bishop and his two assistants were soon submerged into the usual rhythms of church administration; office life quickly adjusted. Deeper analysis however gave hints of developing friction. In this situation, Father Adrian was the least affected. He could work in any environment; he had absorbed interests outside the Church of England, played the clarinet to a high standard and enjoyed all kinds of classical music. He could happily immerse himself in concerts, operas and recitals in the evenings and at weekends.

It was Rev John who was affected the most by the changes. A lonely man with only a few friends, he was given to long periods of self-analysis, and he started to worry deeply about the changes happening around him. With the arrival of Bryan and Jude, he felt as if he had been demoted within the diocese. The bishop's door in spite of earlier promises was never open to him now as it had been during the occupancy of the previous incumbent. So whereas he used to eat a sandwich for lunch at his desk in case the bishop needed to consult him, now instead he wandered outside alone exploring the many narrow streets and courtyards of the City. On his walks, John inevitably found himself looking into old churches in the Square Mile.

At first, he told himself that visits to such churches as St Margaret Lothbury, St Lawrence Jewry, St Helens Bishopsgate and St Botolphs Aldersgate were made to enjoy the architecture, history and general historical ambience of the place, as well as a way of avoiding, however briefly, the new restrictive environment pervading the diocesan offices. All this was true but increasingly he found himself staying for services of Holy Communion and then often returning day by day. After work, he would sit, think and often pray in a church on his way to the tube station for the journey home.

His inner life was changing. He had trained originally as a priest but inevitably his duties in the diocese had taken him away from his calling and submerged him in an atmosphere of bureaucracy and office politics. That development now started to concern him. And he began to ponder if his recent pursuit of money for the diocese over the sale of St Mary Abchurch was perhaps adversely affecting him. Even the very vocabulary of finance now seemed to be always in his thoughts. He knew for a Christian minister this must be wrong, and he decided that he must withdraw from church bureaucracy as soon as practicable and return to his priestly calling.

These changes in his approach to life were noticed by others. Recently he had overheard one of the secretaries whisper to her colleague, "Just not as arrogant as he used to be, and he never chats or whistles about the place anymore."

And then he had found that letter from the Rev Aubrey Braithwaite which had been left in St Mary Abchurch. Even before he opened it, seeing the envelope had brought back all his previous memories of having to deal with that old clergyman. Aubrey, having joined the diocese just before his retirement, had annoyed John with his excuses, his unwillingness to join in anything being organised by the diocese, and his refusal to use modern services. He was a relic the Church of England was desperately trying to be rid of or so he had thought. And his wife, the daughter of a dean or archdeacon, was such a snob it was said.

But, later, when Aubrey had left St Mary Abchurch, John had felt deeply guilty. Thinking about it he had realised that the vicar of St Mary Abchurch was just an old man, a deeply Christian old man, trying to do his best as he had been taught. Furthermore, John would now be the first to admit that he had never actually met Joan his wife and had only based his dislike of her on prejudiced rumour and gossip. After Aubrey and Joan had been forced into early retirement from the church, many members of the congregation from St Mary Abchurch had written to the bishop expressing their support for Aubrey and their disgust and disapproval of the way they thought he and Joan had been misused. John had collected a large file bulging with the correspondence.

One lady he remembered had been particularly abusive in an email about the way Aubrey had been treated and, John remembered, she had ended her missive by complaining about him, Rev John and Father Adrian, and she had said that after a lifetime in the Church of England, she would now nourish her Christian faith with the Methodists. At the time, John had been upset that the lady had bothered to find out the names of clergymen such as himself who worked in the diocesan offices, and he had decided to keep this email and most of the other correspondence away from the bishop.

After the visit to St Mary Abchurch with TPL, John had taken Aubrey Braithwaite's letter home to read it secretly. He had half thought that if it was unpleasant he would just destroy it without telling anyone in the office. No one had seen him remove it that afternoon, and it was very unlikely that Aubrey Braithwaite himself would ever return to the City of London to follow it up.

Later at home, however, he soon forgot his first thought of burning the letter. He sat down to open it after dinner, and its contents immediately distressed him deeply. It was written by hand in ink apparently with an old-fashioned fountain pen and covered several sheets of paper. Aubrey, the vicar, had obviously taken many hours to plan and write it. In the letter, he described his life, his poor upbringing and his feeling of being a failure until, right at the end of his life, he had come to St Mary Abchurch and things had changed.

He talked of ministers educated at university who used their learning to ridicule him. He spoke of not really understanding much of the modern marketing jargon they habitually used. But in spite of these thoughts his sojourn at Abchurch had transformed everything in his life and at last even brought him and Joan closer together; Abchurch was, he had written, a bright shaft of Christian light shining in the City of London which had given him a hint of the future love of heaven.

John reflected that the painted ceiling must have been as much of an influence on Aubrey as it had been on him. This church, Aubrey informed the next vicar, was a saintly place which had changed and enriched not only the lives of him and his wife Joan but also of many other parishioners. He cautioned the next incumbent not to trust the diocese, and Rev John and Father Adrian were mentioned in particular, but just to open the church doors, put a Christian pennant on the building and people would search him out.

Aubrey went on to mention the dozens of people who now enjoyed being a part of St Mary Abchurch. He talked a lot about the old prayer book and the King James Bible and suggested the next vicar should set up regular bible classes to help younger people understand and enjoy these classics of yesteryear which were still highly relevant today and would be for all time. In the end, he gave a list of the names and email addresses of many regular communicants at the church. And he suggested that the new incumbent should set up a proper church council with wardens and other officials right from the start.

The pressure of so much work he explained had been a growing problem for both him and his wife. And, finally, he gave his blessing to a vicar not yet appointed. From the contents of the letter, John could clearly see that Aubrey just assumed that St Mary Abchurch would continue into the future as it had flourished in the past. His ministry was but one mark on the church's long long path of Christian life and work. Clearly, that is what he had assumed.

John read and reread the letter several times in the coming days until he could almost recite it word for word. He decided not to take it into the office to show to others especially Bryan, whom he knew would use it against him with Bishop Leo. He put it away with his private papers hidden at home.

Back in the diocese, legal matters concerning the sale of Rev Aubrey's church were now rushing to their inevitable conclusion. The destruction of St Mary Abchurch just could not be halted. Thoughtful Properties Ltd had decided to construct a street plan of the area of the City around Cannon Street, King William Street and Sherborne Lane. For this task, they had employed a marketing company to make two models, a small one showing the area as it was at the moment and a second larger and more complex model demonstrating the preposed rebirth of the streets and lanes off Cannon Street after the removal of St Mary Abchurch and its substitution with the proposed new Abchurch Tower block.

The chairman outlined more of the details of the plans that week over dinner with Bishop Leo at the House of Lords.

"Are you sure we need two models?" questioned Bishop Leo as he listened. "Won't that just lead to more questions and criticism of the whole scheme? Wouldn't it be better just to ignore the current church and concentrate on the glorious future of this part of London?"

"Well," said the chairman pensively, "the board did indeed consider making just one model but in the end decided that two would give the project added authority. Before and after so to speak. The first model will show a windswept eyesore in need of serious expenditure but the bigger second model will show modern streets and the square with our modest tower phased into it. The top can be taken off the tower entrance hall in the bigger model so the public will see a tiny representation of the beautifully cleaned reredos in front of which we will have our Evensong services. I'm very glad Rev John originally suggested such an idea by the way, please pass my thanks to him for the concept. And Bishop, before I forget, I hope that you will conduct our first Evensong service there as well as formally opening and dedicating the new tower in due course."

Bishop Leo beamed, "Of course, I would be only too pleased to dedicate the building and run the Evensong as well. It will give me the chance to wear one of those spectacular copes the diocese has stored away. Thank you for asking me."

"Please do wear something colourful, Bishop," laughed the chairman. "Anyway," he continued, "the model will show the lifts with the painted ceiling cut up into strips and mounted in glass frames on the walls and the pelican, I think it is, prominently placed over the reception desk."

"The what?" asked Leo.

The chairman laughed, "Apparently, I'm told there is a pelican or some sort of huge bird which you might let us have for our entrance hall. A real talking point for the new building! Rev John I believe is going to ask you about it."

"Oh yes, of course, Bryan did mention it. Only too pleased to let TPL find a purpose for it," said the bishop, "not much use to us at the moment. It can symbolise our new working partnership."

The chairman thanked him and continued, "The religious names of the lifts will be displayed prominently. My marketing people tell me names like Matins, Litany and Hymn have finally been decided upon. It's a much better idea than just numbering them as I'm sure you will agree. The receptionist will direct customers to the Matins or Hymn lift as appropriate.

"Then, in the larger model, we will have tiny figures to represent the staff and the general public dotted around the foyer and out into Abchurch Yard. It's all quite an imaginative idea as I hope you will agree. Do we need another bottle of the New Zealand Sauvignon Blanc or shall we move to the red?"

"Let's stay with the Sauvignon but just a half bottle I think," said Bishop Leo. "I can never get to sleep at night after too much wine. By the way," he continued, "who are you proposing to invite to the presentation? Have your marketing people given it any thought?"

"Actually, I did hope that you could advise me on that bishop," said the chairman. "We have booked the Old Guildhall Library for the event, right in the centre of the City of London. I will introduce the occasion of course then Austin and Eric from the sales side will take over and describe the religious history of the area of Cannon Street with special emphasis on our growing relationship with the Church of England. Then, we might have a question and answer session. After this, I will unveil the models and invite guests to come up to the podium to look at them in detail.

"We will have journalists from the various trade publications as well as the national press, some MPs and government ministers of course, a few clerics and the general public with an emphasis on people associated with the City of London. What do you think? Should we invite the general public or not? And, oh, yes, I nearly forgot that we are giving out sandwiches and a glass of wine to people as they wander around the models. Our marketing people may also produce key rings in the shape of the new tower as a gift for everyone. And, at the end of the whole presentation, we will announce that we are giving a substantial sum to the Archbishop of Canterbury's inner city appeal. The board is about to finalise the actual amount."

"I'm not sure I can add much. You've thought of every angle," said Bishop Leo. "I may ask the Archbishop's staff at Lambeth Palace for their thoughts though. And yes, you need to invite the general public. Don't leave yourself open to charges of trying to conceal anything. By the way, my assistants are looking at the official Grade One aspect of the existing church and how quickly we can get around the regulations."

"Ah, thank you," said the chairman, "that's very much appreciated."

He continued, "The final version of the two models should be ready at the end of the week, and they will be sent to your office in the first instance so that you and your staff can suggest changes or alert us to anything we have omitted. We intend then to set them up in the Guildhall Old Library ready for presentation day."

The warm surroundings of the House of Lords, the chatter of conversation in the dining room and the delicious white wine all made the evening very successful indeed. And discussion later turned naturally to family and personal matters.

"Do you and your wife like the ballet or the opera?" the chairman asked. "I ask because the company has permanent access each night to four seats at Covent Garden, and my wife and I would love to have you both join us for an evening. Some of their productions are truly spectacular."

The bishop glowed, "We don't get to the theatre very often, but we do watch any opera that comes onto the television. I can tell you though that my wife Dorothy does especially love the ballet, although in our busy working lives, opportunities to see it are very limited."

"That's settled then," said the chairman. "A ballet at Covent Garden it is. My secretary will be in touch with you on the details."

By ten o'clock, Bishop Leo was ready to find his chauffeur for the journey home. He was feeling very happy with the way life was developing in his short time in his new diocese. He had now spoken in two debates in parliament and although irritatingly neither the national press nor the BBC or Independent Television had reported on his words, he had been told that his fellow bishops and the archbishops in particular valued his comments. He had met many people in the Lords whom he could now count as friends and colleagues. And he was about to put his personal mark on a major rejuvenation of the City of London.

The Abchurch Tower would dominate the City end of London Bridge for decades into the future. It might indeed be named after him. He imagined with some excitement how he would act as a guide to the two models soon to be on show at the Guildhall Old Library. As the car purred on towards his home in Richmond, the New Zealand Sauvignon Blanc made him feel both externally relaxed and inwardly excited at the same time.

Chapter 5
St Mary Abchurch's
Congregation

The previous vicar at St Mary Abchurch, Aubrey Braithwaite, and his wife Joan, the troublesome couple referred to by Rev John, had departed from the church just before Christmas two years before. Their leaving had been a shock and a disappointment for all parishioners. It had happened so suddenly, with little warning. Yes, there had been rumours for several weeks about them going but that was all. Aubrey was an old man, but he was still a few years away from 70, the official Church of England retirement age.

The congregation at Abchurch had assumed that his popularity and his obvious achievements as a minister would be appreciated at senior levels within the Church of England. After all, during his incumbency at St Mary Abchurch, he had been so successful as a minister. Someone indeed had said that Aubrey's church had become the Piccadilly Circus of the Anglican Communion. He had built up a large congregation of weekday communicants and, unusually for the City of London, had started Sunday services of Matins and Evensong. Because of Aubrey, the church had assumed a central role in the lives of many people from a wide geographical area and even for the drinkers at the Vintry public house next door.

Aubrey and Joan would often be found chatting in the Vintry over a glass or two of cream sherry after Divine Service. The diocese must surely realise that this sort of minister would be vital for the future of the Established Church, especially in a deeply secular age which had appeared to eschew things religious. It was therefore obvious to everyone that Aubrey and Joan would not be allowed to leave, or if allowed to depart would be rapidly rehired.

So it was a serious shock for most parishioners when on the last Sunday of the year many of them had appeared for the usual service of 11:00 am matins only to find the main door locked and notices on it saying the building was now closed and the diocese was not going to replace the vicar. Aubrey would therefore be the last in a series of incumbents extending all the way back to the seventeenth century when Sir Christopher Wren had designed the building. There had been no explanation from the ecclesiastical authorities and no provision for an interim incumbent. The building was just closed permanently and padlocked. The notice had gone on to name other local churches which might be of interest to the existing communicants of St Mary Abchurch.

On that Sunday, standing in the cold December morning, a few of the congregation had burst into tears, partly at the way Aubrey and Joan had been so shabbily treated but also at the abrupt manner in which they as loyal church members had been abandoned. A small group of them agreed there in the churchyard that they would write to the bishop to express their shock that such a development could even happen let alone take place unannounced and without consultation in the modern Church of England. Many also started regularly to write to Aubrey and Joan, trying to keep them both at the front of their lives.

Over the following months, several from this congregation maintained contact with each other and formed an impromptu group which would socialise occasionally at the Vintry pub. They would watch what was happening at their old church and exchange messages as to who was going into the building and how long they stayed. Some also did try to familiarise themselves with other nearby City churches, as the closure notice suggested. Karen and Nancy, two of Rev Aubrey's original communicants, in particular, visited a few local churches, which usually used modern forms of church service, and they made serious attempts to adapt to them. But such efforts produced no real success.

They found little to hold their attention. One lunchtime, walking back to the office after a Holy Communion service at yet another church, Karen said, "You know, Nancy, if I'm honest I am not really inspired by any of the services we attend. I sometimes think it must be my fault. The words are so bland and tepid if words can actually be described as 'tepid'. I can never even remember them a few seconds after I've said them. I only hope God can," she smiled.

"I must tell you that I have taken to reading the Communion Service from the Book of Common Prayer when I get home after work. I just feel that helps the development of my faith so much more than any of these lunchtime services we go to."

"Well, it's interesting you say that," agreed Nancy, "our old vicar, Rev Braithwaite, gave me a copy of the prayer book, so I could look over the marriage service before my wedding at St Mary Abchurch nearly two years ago. And, in all the confusion and rush of getting married, I forgot to return it to him. My husband and I have occasionally read the matins service from it on a Sunday morning rather than actually finding a church to go to.

"In an odd way, we both find reading those words from Thomas Cranmer more fulfilling than some of what we hear read out in church these days. And I also find his services easier to remember. There is a rhythm and poetry to the words. And repeating such well-known phrases over the weeks helps my faith if I'm truthful."

Karen readily agreed. "You are so right Nancy. I was rather hoping that we could find somewhere in the City of London to hear the old prayer book, and I know that one or two churches here do use it, but rumour says the new bishop does not like Thomas Cranmer and all that he stood for. So I imagine these few churches are not likely to survive long. I guess that's that. We have to arrange our own services at home as far as we can of course."

"Oh, by the way," said Nancy, "I saw a poster in a shop in Cannon Street about a meeting in the Guildhall. Apparently, now, they are going to knock down our dear old church and replace it with one of those ugly modern towers. The details will be announced there and that new bishop you mentioned is supposed to turn up. Let's go along, I'm sure we can get the afternoon off from work. In fact, why don't we take a few of our friends from the old Abchurch congregation and some of the patrons of the Vintry with us to give support? I walked near St Mary Abchurch at the weekend. Have you seen it in the last few days?"

"I've seen the wooden awning," said Karen.

"Well, the story gets worse," continued Nancy. "Best to stay away I would advise. You will start crying. That awning is bad enough but some vandals have now sprayed it all with yellow paint. It all looks quite dreadful.

"I'm pleased Aubrey and Joan aren't here to see it. I sometimes feel that I must be asleep and dreaming some kind of nightmare. No one from the diocese seems to care. Our Vintry group wants to write to the Archbishop about it by the way. They have given up bothering with the bishop down at St Paul's. We all wrote to him complaining about the treatment metered out to Aubrey, and he never acknowledged our letters or indeed bothered to reply."

The two young ladies arranged to attend the meeting in the Guildhall and managed to interest some from the former Sunday matins congregation as well as a few drinkers from the Vintry pub who remembered Mr and Mrs Vicar with great affection.

Chapter 6
Guildhall, the Old Library

Early in June, the contract of sale between the Diocese of London and TPL was finally ready for signing. Last-minute glitches had been ironed out. The Guildhall Old Library had been booked for a presentation of the proposals to all interested parties. An extravagant spread of food and wine had been prepared, and a bronze key ring, featuring a miniature Abchurch Tower, was ready to be given to everyone as they arrived. At the centre of the proceedings were the two models of Abchurch Yard, one showing a rundown, windswept existing church which was boarded up and daubed with graffiti and the other highlighting the potential glorious future for this part of a redeveloped city, close as it is to Cannon Street, London Bridge and London Bridge Station.

The company was not sure how much interest their talk might attract so a generous arrangement of chairs had been set up. At the front on a raised dais had been placed a table with chairs for the board and for Bishop Leo and his assistants Bryan and Jude. An extravagant display of spring flowers placed in the middle of the dais gave a warm and friendly aspect to the whole proceedings.

The chairman had assured Bishop Leo that all would be well. Thoughtful Properties Ltd often made such presentations in many cities throughout Great Britain. They understood how to make the day successful and how to smooth over any difficult questions and comments. They even had a mock presentation room set up in company headquarters where the board had been able to rehearse the event, rather in the way that TPL staff usually practised for the annual general meetings. On this occasion, however, unfortunately, matters did not proceed in the way they had been meticulously planned.

The doors were opened at half past two on that June afternoon and rather surprisingly within fifteen minutes all the available chairs were full. And, by the time of the start of the presentation at three o'clock, many people were having to stand, confined uncomfortably in pressed rows at the sides and the rear.

"My goodness," whispered the chairman to Bishop Leo, "I never expected this sort of interest. They are really crowding in. Perhaps we should have booked a bigger room." And he quietly murmured a few words of warning to the other board members.

The bishop just returned him a watery smile and said nothing. In truth, however, seeing the size of the attendance, he was starting to feel very nervous to the pit of his stomach. He now realised with some horror that he wasn't really prepared for such a meeting. Bryan and Jude had told him that no one was very much interested in St Mary Abchurch.

He had merely taken their word and had repeated their assurances to the chairman. He hadn't even had the time himself actually to see the church as events in the House of

Lords were taking so much of his waking hours. He leant over to Bryan, "Bryan, when you and Jude looked inside this old church, how did it appear to you?"

Bryan frowned, "Well, actually neither of us has had the time to get to the church. We did mean to look inside it the other day, but we were working on your second speech for the Lords, you might remember," he replied disingenuously.

"But you both have seen it from the outside at least, surely?" said Bishop Leo now feeling quite agitated. "Do please assure me of that."

Bryan and Jude looked at each other and then admitted that they had not actually been near the place. They explained that they had foolishly got lost in the many small city streets on the day of their planned visit. Jude however discreetly produced an old twentieth-century Guide to the City of London churches from his briefcase. "But we do have this," he whispered, "a quick prompt might help us all perhaps."

"You do realise this meeting starts in two minutes, two minutes, and I will be expected to endorse this complicated and no doubt controversial proposal, and then later sign a major contract, and I now find that all three of us are in the dark about the very building at the centre of it all, St Mary Abchurch. Quick, what does that guidebook say?" The bishop now was not only starting to perspire but was also having some difficulty controlling his growing anger.

Jude rapidly skimmed the relevant pages and frowned.

"Well," Bishop Leo almost shouted. "It's virtually three o'clock. What does it say?"

"Oh, dear, not necessarily good news I'm afraid. It starts by stating that St Mary Abchurch is one of the finest and most imaginative churches ever built by Sir Christopher Wren, himself the most famous architect England has produced," said Jude who was also now starting to feel uncomfortable. "The rest of the blurb talks about a painted dome and a wooden reredos by Grinling Gibbons the well-known wood and stone carver."

"You two did consult Rev John and Father Adrian I suppose, as I distinctly remember asking you to do, the two people who know the most about this whole project and indeed about the City of London?"

Bryan and Jude said nothing, both looking down and fidgeting with the programme. Bryan eventually apologised and said that he was having problems because the flowers on the table were starting his hay fever.

Bishop Leo tried to stay calm in front of what was now a very busy Guildhall Old Library. His thoughts which previously had been drifting away to the House of Lords, were now sharply concentrated on events unfolding in the room before him. He looked down at his copy of the meeting schedule. Yes, there was as he imagined there would be, a large opportunity for questions and answers. He, Bishop Leo, would obviously need to field many and no doubt all religious questions from the floor, and he could see that several clerical collars were dotted around amongst the audience.

The clergy would undoubtedly be interested in what he had to say and some would probably pose awkward comments about destroying churches and suchlike. This morning he had been so looking forward to this presentation. He had assumed he would walk around the models and talk a bit about the developing Church of England within the City of London all washed down with a few glasses of red wine. Instead matters might rapidly turn unpleasant, he realised that now. And no doubt the evening newspaper, sensing an embarrassing story would give the proceedings maximum publicity. In his panic, he imagined that the audience could see just how much he was perspiring.

Three o'clock chimed on a long-case clock at the front of the room. The chairman smiled, stood up, welcomed everyone and introduced those on the platform individually by name. He then explained that TPL wanted to redevelop the City end of London Bridge including Abchurch Yard in order to create a world-class entrance to London for everyone walking over the bridge from London Bridge Station. This set the scene. London was always associated in the popular mind with London Bridge, so this new project would tie the Abchurch area for all time firmly to the Bridge itself.

He pressed a button and the room lights were turned down, a large screen appeared from the ceiling and a short video was shown that cleverly highlighted the new TPL tower and emphasised how it would phase naturally into the local area, giving dignity and gravitas both to Abchurch Yard and Abchurch Lane. The stone supports in the tower would match and complement many of the prominent buildings in this part of the historic City of London. The video described the pieces from the church which would be displayed in the new tower. The film was accompanied by a sensitive rendering of Handel's Water Music played by a prominent London orchestra.

The chairman quipped when the video ended, "Handel was not a native of London but Londoners quickly adopted him as one of their own. The new Abchurch Tower would, although new, likewise be adopted by Londoners in time and become as much a part of the Square Mile as was the Bank of England or St Paul's Cathedral."

The chairman then introduced Austin and Eric from the sales subsidiary who described at length the company's new relationship with the Church of England and the ongoing small investment by the diocese in the proposed development. They underlined the worrying structural dangers of St Mary Abchurch where the foundations were very shallow, and they spoke of retaining the artefacts from the building inside the new tower block and made particular emphasis on the font cover, reredos and pulpit door which would be kept in the new entrance hall along with pieces from the painted dome which would find a place in the main lifts. And both men made a special point about the proposed annual Evensong.

The chairman then followed this with a technical description of the new tower and explained how it would advance the engineering and computer skills of his company and indeed of the country as well. The London Underground railway and a major sewer both ran under the site so constructing a new tower around and over them would be especially challenging. Copies of various drawings were passed out around the room to demonstrate both the problems and TPL's proposed answers to them. By a quarter to four, the chairman and the whole board were starting to feel more relaxed. The meeting was going to plan, there really was no need for Leo to be concerned.

"Now," the chairman announced, "before we look around the two models, we have prepared to show you, which we can do whilst we have a few sandwiches and some wine, it is time for a question and answer session where we can hear your thoughts, ladies and gentlemen. Oh, and I nearly forgot as part of our new relationship with the Church of England the Board of TPL will be making a substantial donation to the Archbishop of Canterbury's inner city appeal scheme. Details of the amount and the Archbishop's proposals are in a separate leaflet." He then sat down.

Several hands quickly shot up from all sides of the library. Bishop Leo noticed with alarm that clerics were predominantly the ones who wanted to speak. Although this was billed as a presentation from Thoughtful Properties Ltd, he guessed it would be the representatives from the Church of England who found themselves under attack, not the chairman and his colleagues. And he was of course correct. Questions and comments were focussed with rapid-fire, particularly on the bishop.

How could the Anglican faith progress if it merely closed its churches? Didn't the bishop realise just how important such a building was as it was designed by Wren? Why was it significant to have one service of Evensong a year in the new tower when there could be at least one a week in the existing structure? Were we repeating the idiocy of the Victorians by bulldozing the past? Had we forgotten why tourists actually came to look at the City of London each year?

Has the church surrendered totally to the dictates of mammon rather than the needs of God? Why has the government allowed the laws associated with Grade One property to be so overruled? Was it intended to transact other similar deals with Thoughtful Properties Ltd all in the interest of finance?

One American lady in the audience asked why the diocese couldn't sell the church to the Americans if all it needed was money. She pointed out to emphasise her point that St Mary the Virgin, Aldermanbury had been taken from the City of London and rebuilt in Fulton, Missouri after the last war. The mention of yet another St Mary made Bryan visibly shake his head. The questions and comments gushed forth in a ceaseless torrent.

Bishop Leo could barely answer one before the next one was shouted out. The chairman sat silently making a few notes. If he did occasionally participate it was only to ask the audience to pose questions courteously and give the bishop time to reply.

Bishop Leo desperately tried to answer as much as possible. He told the audience that old pews would be donated to poor parishes in Africa. It was important for English Anglicans to support churches in poorer parts of the world. He reassured the assembled clerics that there were no plans to sell off other churches. He was adamant that the Church of England had great plans for expansion in London, and indeed that is why they wanted the funds.

The sale proceeds would be used to train young men and women who wanted a career in the ministry and to help repair and expand existing churches. And it was so important that those present today appreciated the fact that much of the interior of St Mary Abchurch would actually be saved as Austin and Eric had already explained. The beautiful reredos would be cleaned and put up in the foyer of the new building which was of course on the site of St Mary Abchurch itself; even significant pieces of the famous painted ceiling would have a long-term future.

After the bishop had said these last words, several people sitting together in the middle of the room noisily and prominently got to their feet and uninvited paraded around the models and then to the back of the room and straight out of the library. Bishop Leo looked on in amazement. The group was silent but an observant bystander might have noticed Karen and Nancy with several from the congregation who used to worship regularly at St Mary Abchurch. Two women amongst them were obviously in tears. As they reached the door, Nancy turned round and from the back of the room shouted to those standing nearby, "And to think I was married in St Mary Abchurch only the year before last before it became an office block."

By half past four, the chairman had decided to move the meeting on. He stood up and said time was getting on and everyone must have a chance to see the models and have a glass or two of wine. He could see that several hands were still raised, so he and Bishop Leo would stay around until six o'clock to answer any remaining questions. And if anyone felt they had been ignored they could email their comments to his secretary whose details were available on the meeting agenda.

Most of the audience then jostled around the two models, leaving dirty finger marks over both, after which there was the inevitable stampede for the wine, sandwiches and crisps.

Bryan and Jude had been very quiet during the question and answer session, even when Bishop Leo had been faltering and obviously looking for verbal support they had said nothing. They both had merely prayed inwardly that no one from the audience pointed at either of them when asking a question. They anticipated correctly as it turned out that the bishop's ire would be focussed on them later that evening or tomorrow morning. Jude in particular knew this would be the case because when later he interrogated his social media account he found dozens of posts describing a confused bishop out of his depth and very much alone, obviously unsupported by his assistants, as he tried to sell off some of the City of London's 'crown jewels'.

At six o'clock, the meeting came to an end. Most people had already left and the few stragglers were persuaded to follow them. The chairman, still uncharacteristically silent, then walked across to Bishop Leo.

"Fancy another dinner in the Lords, or do you have other plans?" he said.

The bishop, still visibly sweating, thought that was a very good idea and both the senior men went out and got into his chauffeur-driven car.

"I think we have a lot to talk about," said the chairman curtly.

In the car for the drive to parliament, neither of the men spoke. Even the chauffeur sensing an atmosphere remained silent. During the journey, the chairman sent and received various text messages on his mobile phone. Bishop Leo merely sat fidgeting with his clerical collar. On arrival at the House of Lords, the pair walked quickly to the Peers' Dining Room where a reserved quiet corner table was already awaiting them.

After both men had placed their orders for dinner, the chairman spoke first.

"Look Bishop," he said, "please don't take this personally but in all my years at TPL and in all the meetings I have attended I have never been so embarrassed and frankly disturbed during a public gathering. And I thought we had rehearsed it so well. Whoever were all those people who just got up and walked out even before I had invited the public to look over the models? I did notice as I'm sure you did that many in the room seemed to be clergymen and women by the way. I assume that you didn't know them.

"In that entire question and answer session, no one actually spoke about our new tower block. And that was the whole point of the meeting. Instead, it was all about the Church of England destroying a well-loved historic church. I just sat there with nothing to say. I tried to think how I might intervene to support you, but frankly, I was stumped."

Bishop Leo started to speak in reply but the chairman indicated he wanted to say more.

"If I understand the gist of my text messages which I was reading in the car just now, many of our board think that TPL appears to be, how can I express it, on the wrong side of history on this. I thought we were reinvigorating the rundown area to the north end of London Bridge. Perhaps I was being naive. Frankly, some of my board feel that we've been dragged involuntarily into a project which, after all, was an idea which came I believe from the Church of England in the first place. Furthermore, I've had several negative comments from major shareholders.

"My contacts at the stock exchange have also been in touch to say that our shares will dive when the market opens tomorrow morning. And when our share price drops suddenly then the board takes note and is forced to respond. The stock exchange will demand a statement. Don't worry I'm not saying that we will suddenly drop our relationship with the church," he said seeing the look of alarm on Bishop Leo's face. "But you must appreciate my predicament, and after all, you, the bishop and the diocese will get bad press too.

"I think both our institutions need to be in damage limitation mode. I'm too anxious about the whole situation to think clearly and to discuss this further tonight. But I warn you I do need to take a serious sounding from the board before we at TPL make any further moves. Anyway, we are going to the Royal Opera House next week. The event will give us both a suitable pause to consider all options. Enough for tonight. Enjoy your steak and this interesting bottle of red wine, which I see heading towards us."

Bishop Leo nodded his agreement and the two men finished their dinner in embarrassed silence.

Chapter 7
Demonstration in the Cathedral

The following day Karen and Nancy entered St Paul's Cathedral and walked slowly up the main aisle to join the tourists and a few locals for the daily service of Evensong. They carried between them a large carrier bag. Nancy's husband, supporting a heavy satchel over his shoulder, followed them a few minutes later. No one particularly noticed the three as they took service sheets and found places near the front in a prominent position under the dome. Each however was starting to perspire even though the cathedral was not especially warm that early summer afternoon.

"I'm really quite nervous you know," whispered Nancy to her friend as she sat down. "I'm very much a law-abiding person. I've never done such a thing before. I didn't even go on a demonstration when I was at uni." She looked around apologetically at the slowly filling cathedral. "It's all so very public," she sighed.

"No changing our minds now," said Karen firmly. "Sometimes in life someone has to say 'No'. We will register our protest at least. Make our views known. The press may hear about it, remember.

"And if what we do today gives us a police record well so be it. That model which those businessmen had of Abchurch Yard after its redevelopment really upset me. I couldn't get to sleep later after we saw it in the Guildhall if I'm truthful. I kept tossing about and thinking of our poor old vicar and his wife and all those kindnesses he showed us, and his reflective sermons and the lovely music that Bob used to play. And I thought of the countless people who have worshipped there for hundreds of years in our stunningly beautiful church.

"These new plans are just awful. If Sir Christopher Wren has a ghost it must be wandering about the earth in some distress. Fancy cutting up that amazing dome just to put pieces into the sides of a few lifts. And who, except for a madman, could possibly dream of fixing the font cover and pulpit door inside a glass case or of putting Grinling Gibbons' amazing reredos inside a tower block and pretending it was preserving the spirit of the church, no matter how much it had been cleaned.

"How can you hold an Evensong service, such as the one here now, in the foyer of an office building? It makes no sense. And then that idea of giving the pews to a church abroad made me almost physically sick even if it did make that sanctimonious bishop feel self-righteous. No, no going back now."

"Yes, you are right," whispered Nancy her resolve suitably stiffened, "I agree, it's something we have to do. Can you imagine me years from now showing my grandchildren where I was married and all they can see is a pulpit door in a glass case or a pelican perched over an information desk? That plan for the pelican made me very cross. How that company could even think such an idea linked their monstrosity of a building with St Mary Abchurch and its Christian past? And as for giving each of us a key ring of the new tower. Rubs salt in the wound I thought. I dropped mine in the litter bin outside the Guildhall."

The organ suddenly started to boom loudly. Choir and clergy, formally robed in cassock and surplice, processed in an orderly fashion into the cathedral. The congregation, by now quite sizeable in number and dispersed over several rows, came to its feet ready to begin.

As soon as the clergy had taken their allotted seats, the age-old familiar words of the Book of Common Prayer followed. Sins were admitted and subsequently forgiven; responses were chanted; the Lord's Prayer was said and a few short verses of the psalm appointed for the day were sung. All those present then sat down to listen to the words of the first lesson taken as usual from the Old Testament, and on this occasion from the story of Noah in the Book of Genesis.

At that moment, as they had worked out over several afternoons, taking the reading as a signal, Nancy and Karen calmly stood up, took a large banner from their bag, moved out to the front of the nave and held it high up on poles which they screwed together whilst facing the congregation. The banner boldly proclaimed in vivid red paint on a white background the legend 'Save St Mary Abchurch from the Philistines'. Karen had brought along a powerful loudhailer, and she started to scream the same reprise through it. At the same time, Nancy's husband walked calmly down the rows of chairs and passed out piles of handbills from his satchel, which contained an expanded message on the same theme. The leaflets were duly passed along by the congregation who assumed at first that they were part of the service.

No one in authority knew how to react, and in truth, it took a few moments before the clergy and congregation realised that such an interruption was not part of Evensong. But then when the chanting became louder and louder, the scene turned into one of pandemonium. The words of the Bible were lost. The first lesson was abandoned in the uproar and the officiating clergyman returned to his seat. Noah was left building his ark.

One of the clergy shouted urgently for the security men, many of whom were taking a tea break now that the service had begun. Several of the choir started to laugh and giggle and, some enjoying the interruption, roared their approval and clapped the women, in spite of the anger of the choirmaster. Two of the younger choir boys then took advantage of the fuss to rush forward, grab the leaflets and start throwing them in all directions. "Don't worry," laughed one, "we will put this up on social media later. Wow, you ladies are really superb! We shall get into trouble I'm sure, but what a hoot!"

The dean's assistant then shouted for someone to fetch the police. Evensong of course was forgotten, except by the organist, who thought he could restore some sort of order by playing the Magnificat very loudly. His contribution however only added to the chaos of the scene. In all this melee, Nancy and Karen never faltered. They kept loudly shouting, "Save St Mary Abchurch from the Philistines."

Some of the tourists, glad to see that what they assumed to be English eccentricity was still in evidence, came up and dropped notes and coins into Karen's bag and posed for selfies standing beside her. Several tourists saved the handbills as mementos and later two visitors asked Nancy to autograph their copies. Many enterprising local residents were videoing the scene on their smartphones, hoping to sell copies to the television evening news.

The uproar couldn't continue of course. Clergymen rushed about trying to collect up and destroy the dozens of leaflets now scattered over a large area of the nave. At this point, several policemen and women rushed into the cathedral, and after herding up, the three protesters quickly escorted them and their equipment outside and down the main steps. Eventually, they were held together in front of the building near the statue of Queen Anne.

"As if we don't have enough to deal with," said one inspector to his sergeant. "Breach of the peace. Just take their details and book them to appear before the magistrate tomorrow morning. Fancy defiling a religious place like a cathedral!"

At that moment, quite unexpectedly, Rev John appeared. He had decided to attend Evensong that day even though usually he had little sympathy for prayer book services. The sale of St Mary Abchurch was now starting to trouble him deeply particularly as the date for signing the contract was approaching. In fact, many recent events associated with Thoughtful Properties were now disturbing his sleep. That letter from the Revd Aubrey Braithwaite had upset him more than he liked to admit and today he had felt the need just to sit in the cathedral to pray and to give himself time to think.

He was wearing his clerical collar and could have joined the officiating clergy but had decided to take his place with the congregation and so had witnessed the entire commotion as it unfolded in front of him that June afternoon. And thinking about it later he started to wonder if his presence in St Paul's Cathedral might have been intended perhaps by higher celestial authority as a way of forcing him to rethink further the way his life had been developing. Truth to tell he felt a twinge of deep sympathy for the earnest young people and increasingly for the plight of St Mary Abchurch. That visit to the property days before had made him realise just how lovely were such Sir Christopher Wren buildings when experienced close-up. And the more he had talked to the representatives of Thoughtful Properties Ltd and been enmeshed in the details of their project for the area, the more he had become at first cross then embarrassed and finally disillusioned with the whole enterprise.

He approached the police cordon. "Look, please just let them go," he said to one of the policemen. "I work here in the main diocesan office, and I can tell you the church won't want to prosecute and in fact will probably want to forget the whole thing as quickly as possible."

"Not as easy as that, padre," said the police sergeant. "This isn't just any old church. It's St Paul's Cathedral. Oh, who told them," he exclaimed as a BBC van pulled up near the kerb. "Move along now," he shouted to the growing crowd of worshippers thronging onto the cathedral steps. "Show's over!"

Many tourists though were obviously not keen to be sent away. Dozens were clapping in obvious support of the young protesters and several shouted objections to their detention, even though few had ever heard of St Mary Abchurch.

Karen, Nancy, and her husband gave their details to the police and were told to report to the magistrate the following day. Their equipment was then forfeited. Released at last to applause from the crowd, they grinned, waved and walked around the cathedral and then slowly up Cannon Street.

Nancy's husband left them and rushed away to have a drink with friends.

"I'm not really sure we did any good in the long run," said Nancy dejectedly as they sauntered along. "They are going to destroy St Mary Abchurch whatever we do. Money talks, especially in a place like the City of London. It's no good fooling ourselves."

"Yes, I suppose you are right," said Karen. "It's sad though. Being realistic I'm not sure what we could possibly do next. Maybe our brief demonstrating days are behind us. Of course, the newspapers may publish something, and I did notice a BBC van there as we were leaving so perhaps the local television news may take up our case."

The two protesters handed out a few leaflets to bewildered commuters who were hurrying towards Cannon Street Station. Further on they then turned into Abchurch Lane and faced the boarded-up church now looking very miserable indeed in the early evening light.

"Look," Karen continued, "let's at least stick some posters up onto the wooden awning around the church. We said we would do that as the second part of our demonstration if you remember." Nancy agreed, and for the next few minutes, the two friends fastened copies of their leaflet to the boards which encased St Mary Abchurch until all the ugly yellow graffiti had been totally covered over.

One of the drinkers popped out from the Vintry pub to watch. "You know you two were just on the early evening television news," he said laughing. "You've become quite famous. I bet they will invite you to be interviewed.

"Television cameras were here filming the building a few minutes ago. You've only just missed them. All the Vintry regulars hope you are going to continue your campaign. We don't want them to destroy our old church. We will contribute a few pounds at least to print more leaflets I'm sure."

"That's so very kind," smiled Nancy. "What you say gives us the strength to go on. Originally we had thought perhaps we could rent a small room somewhere to hold a meeting to advertise our protest and give some publicity to it. But now I'm not sure we could afford to do so."

"Well, why not do that? Actually, why don't I ask the manager here if he would let you use that large space they have downstairs? It's perfect I would think. Don't give up! Please!" said the drinker from the Vintry, sticking his thumb up as a signal of support. "St Mary Abchurch is the very soul of this square."

At that moment, Rev John appeared from around the corner. He had slowly walked up Cannon Street following the two young women. He had decided that he wanted to have a serious chat with them but was unsure how actually to approach them. Walking over he started to read the posters plastered over the wooden awning. It was Karen who approached him first.

"You are the minister who spoke up for us outside St Paul's," she said recognising him. "Thanks for doing that. It was very kind. You look as though you understand what we are trying to do."

"Well, yes, I think I do," he admitted. "Look," he blurted out. "Let me buy you both a drink. If you have the time I feel I want to chat. I followed you both to try and introduce myself."

For the next hour, Rev John sat with Nancy and Karen outside St Mary Abchurch in the early evening sunlight whilst he told them about his involvement with the rebuilding scheme, his doubts about the project and latterly his disillusionment with the whole idea. He admitted he had met the previous vicar, Aubrey, although he didn't give details, and he didn't mention the letter he had found in the church. He thought he might mention this on a later occasion. Warmed by the wine, as the evening became darker he then confessed that this act of destroying the church was leading him to question why he was even in the Church of England at all, in spite of his faith as a Christian.

Nancy and Karen listened quietly and then told John about their involvement with St Mary Abchurch. Nancy told of her wedding there and both women explained how the vicar's lunchtime services of Holy Communion had taken on a pivotal role in both their lives. They described the sense of unhappiness and abandonment they had felt when they had first heard their vicar was retiring early and then again later when they saw the building they loved, boarded-up, windswept and desolate.

By ten o'clock, it was almost totally dark but the three just continued drinking and talking until John said, "I'm always looking to interpret events that happen in my life, and I am starting to feel that meeting both of you is important. It might give me the chance to make amends for some of the silly and hurtful things I have said and done over many recent months. Please let me join your campaign to save this building in front of us. If I can be of any help I mean. Involvement might even help me to settle my mind over many matters."

Nancy and Karen stared at Rev John.

"Okay," said Karen. "I think from what you are saying that you want us to turn our protest into a proper movement.

John, I think you might be the person we are looking for to give it focus. I propose that we say it is now a formal campaign with only one aim. To save St Mary Abchurch from the developers and reopen it as our local church with our own parish vicar."

"Just a minute," broke in Nancy. "I propose we have two aims. I agree with your first aim. But, in addition, our St Mary Abchurch movement has to have a second one, once the church has been saved and reopened we must continue with historic ancient services. Our old vicar married my husband and me according to the Book of Common Prayer and the King James Bible, and he taught us both to appreciate them.

"The prayer book is an amazing work which gives peace to my own life, and I feel that its language keeps our souls in communion with all who have gone before us in this place. If no I mean when we reopen our church, any new vicar must use the prayer book."

John smiled and mouthed silently in the darkness, "The Peace of God which passeth all understand." Out loud he said, "Such an idea would upset our new bishop, the one you saw in the Guildhall. He hates the prayer book and all it stands for. He would say you were CO people. He means folk who are Cranmer Obsessed. Furthermore, I should tell you that such an idea would be a total transformation for me.

"In the past, I've always disliked the Book of Common Prayer. Although if I'm honest I have never actually used it or studied it. My theological college tutors were uniformly hostile to the book. So using it might be good for my soul. If St Mary Abchurch is to continue using the prayer book I guess I might have a lot of reading and learning to do. But yes, why not? I'm with you. Our new protest movement has two clear purposes."

The three friends agreed to the twin aims over a final glass of wine as the evening turned the square totally dark.

"Probably the end of any serious ecclesiastical career I might have enjoyed I suppose," Rev John winced in the darkness, "fighting against TPL and sponsoring the Book of Common Prayer at the same time, both aim totally against the wishes of my bishop."

"Oh, come on," counselled Karen. "This campaign will be the making of each of us. I sense it. And there are many dioceses in the Church of England for you to work in. Let's go into the Vintry and enquire about that meeting room. Perhaps we can fix it for tomorrow whilst we are all so enthusiastic."

Chapter 8
Roderick Scott

The following day, Roderick Scott, a very wealthy, retired businessman from Amity, Arkansas in the United States walked slowly up Cannon St tightly holding a paper map of London given to him that morning at the hotel reception. Map reading was a pursuit he hated; he had no patience to bother with the various symbols and the constant folding and unfolding of the paper smudged the names of the streets and buildings. Olive would have understood how to read the thing, he knew, thinking of his dear wife who had died in London on these same streets not so very long before. He passed the main Cannon Street railway station and heading towards London Bridge crossed the busy thoroughfare near Boots the Chemist and suddenly in front of him there was the sign indicated on his map, the sign he wanted.

There was Abchurch Lane leading to the church of St Mary Abchurch, as written on a rather faded old-fashioned brown sign. He was in luck. The church minister there had been such a help to his wife at the end of her life that Roderick had determined to come to London just to say thank you personally. Today he wanted to surprise him and perhaps offer a good lunch to both him and his wife.

He walked into the lane and immediately entered Abchurch Square. He was by now quite excited, having spent the morning speculating what the vicar would look like. He had decided he must be distinguished with a head of grey bushy hair and his wife dressed as a rather stylish modern consort both heading up a busy ancient English church building. Imagine then his shock at the scene in front of him. Not only was there no minister and his wife to be seen, but there was barely even a church.

A church building of some sort there certainly was. But it was boarded up, rundown, quite derelict and obviously not in use. Large murky windows could be seen protruding above a high wooden awning. *This can't be right*, thought Roderick.

Olive's letter, dictated to a nurse as she was dying, had said clearly that the minister was enthusiastic about his church which he had said was so vibrant and active. And indeed he had received a kind and informative note from that very vicar himself not so many months ago. *This can't be St Mary Abchurch. I'm so hopeless at map reading. I've come the wrong way*, he thought.

He walked further down Abchurch Lane and out into a very busy King William Street. And there he stopped. Yes, he must be right; this was the place she had been taken ill he mused. He remembered the street name, King William, which he had thought so odd. That building really must be St Mary Abchurch.

He walked back to the square and pushed aside the wooden barricade to find a faded notice stapled to the main door. "Yes, it is the right place," he murmured to himself, as he read aloud, "St Mary Abchurch. The building is closed and is under consideration for sale. Please address all interest to the bishop's office by St Paul's Cathedral. Then, there was an address, telephone number and email."

At that moment, a man stacking beer glasses on tables outside the nearby pub, the Vintry, shouted out to him. "Be careful mate there's a mess of all sorts around there. Don't touch anything. You will damage your shoes and clothes. Best stay away."

Roderick walked over to introduce himself. "Well, I wonder if you can help me. I'm a visitor from the United States. This is St Mary Abchurch, I am right," he puzzled.

"Well, it used to be, certainly," said the publican. "You have come to the right place, although for how much longer it will be a church no one knows. As you have probably been told, it's a gem of a place inside, but despite that, it's going to be pulled down and redeveloped. Yet another office block I assume. God only knows why they keep building them. We've had various property types crawling over the place in the last few weeks, so I guess the bulldozers will be crashing through here before too long making all our lives miserable."

"Didn't there used to be a padre, called Aubrey, I think, who ran the place when it was open?" questioned Roderick.

"Yes, that's right, there did," confirmed the publican. "Aubrey Braithwaite and his wife, Joan. A charming couple. Mr and Mrs Vicar we used to call them.

"They knew everyone around here. They filled that place with a stream of churchgoers. They loved cream sherry—the only customers whoever did. There is no call for cream sherry these days, but I had to keep a couple of bottles around just for them. They got forced out suddenly some months ago.

"It was all such a shock. I can't imagine what they did wrong and as you can see, no one has replaced them since.

Several of us wrote complaining about the situation to the bishop, but he never bothered to reply. I don't imagine he even saw the letters. Then, those wooden barricades suddenly appeared one weekend last January."

"Where did they go?" asked Roderick. "Your Mr and Mrs Vicar?"

"I don't remember but some of my regulars might. Have a drink, and I will ask around."

Roderick Scott sat at a vacant table in the yard, folded up his map and drank a glass of beer in the sunshine. He didn't have to wait long. Word soon went around the pub that an American was looking for information on St Mary Abchurch and its previous vicar. Several men and women came out to join him and chat.

Roderick introduced himself and bought a round of drinks for everyone. "I'm rather surprised," he said "I expected to see a busy vibrant chapel with its doors open to welcome all. Instead, I find this. Is it structurally unsound? Has it been closed for safety reasons?"

"Well, you might be forgiven for thinking so," said one of his new friends. "It's a national disgrace, and it was built by Sir Christopher Wren of all people. You couldn't get more famous than him! That notice on the door says it's going to be sold. I'm not sure if that means just the building or the contents or both."

"I hear that the building can't be saved and will just be torn down," said another, "after they have sold off the bits and pieces."

"I just can't get my head around this," said Roderick. "In the United States, such a place would be treated as a national treasure, and the government would pour money into it. But tell me what happened to Aubrey Braithwaite and Joan. He in particular was so very kind to my wife when she was seriously ill and in fact dying just round the corner."

"Oh, we loved Mr and Mrs Vicar," said another. "They often would enjoy a glass of cream sherry with us on long summer evenings. Such good and kind people. And if I might say it, they were Christian folk. Going to church doesn't always mean you are a Christian. But they were, the best sort."

"Well, you know what it's like," interjected another lady. "Face doesn't fit the new breed at head office. All big companies are the same."

"Yes, I know from my own experience that is very true but a Christian church isn't a company and ought to be different somehow," said Roderick frowning. "Can I get inside to look around the place?"

"I don't see why not. We have seen a few people go inside just lately. I would just knock on the bishop's door and ask his secretary for permission," said the first man. "Actually, I did notice some official-looking businessmen going in only the other day. And, by the way, here is the vicar's retirement address in East Anglia." And he wrote the details carefully on the back of a menu card.

Roderick thanked his new friends for their help, finished his beer and moved off back down Cannon St towards St Paul's Cathedral which he could see clearly in the distance. Eventually, he found the bishop's office, knocked on the door, introduced himself to an administrator and explained his mission. He told her about his wife dying in the city and the kindness of the vicar, Aubrey, of St Mary Abchurch and said he would like just to look inside Aubrey's church for a few minutes if that could be arranged.

Thinking about it later he realised that the administrator had been very welcoming at first, but it was when he mentioned the name of the church and also gave Aubrey's name that her demeanour had quickly changed.

"Oh, I see. Just a minute and I will have a word with the bishop," she said rather coldly and disappeared into another office, leaving Roderick standing outside. She returned quickly. "Sorry, I forgot, the bishop is in the House of Lords today but his personal assistant just confirmed what I already knew. It's rather negative and a message you might not want to hear.

"The bishop can't let you into St Mary Abchurch. The place is not safe. There is a wooden awning around the building and government regulations prevent anyone from going inside at the moment. Health and Safety issues you understand." And she started aggressively to shepherd Roderick back towards the gate.

Roderick, who was not used to being fobbed off in such a fashion on any issue, glared at the young lady. He remembered hearing from his wife about the difficulties the minister of St Mary Abchurch had, trying to keep his parish open when faced with diocesan indifference.

"Look, I can sign an indemnity or whatever you call it to say I'm responsible for any accident, not you, and I'm very happy to wear a hard hat or whatever is required," he said. "I've come a long way across the Atlantic, and I really would love to look inside even for just a few minutes. And, of course, I'm also happy to make a substantial contribution to church funds if that would help."

"It's not a matter of money sir," said the administrator dismissively. "If we let you go inside then we would have a stream of other visitors. Our insurance would never allow it, hard hats notwithstanding. The building is officially closed. Moreover, if children went in we would be in the realm of many other difficult issues such as safeguarding."

"Goodness me," exclaimed Roderick, becoming very cross. "Safeguarding! Whatever are you talking about! I'm not a child. Do I look like a child? I just want to see inside St Mary Abchurch for five minutes to experience the place where that kind minister, who was so good to my wife, officiated.

"That's all. Surely you can understand that and appreciate what I am saying. My wife died close by and St Mary Abchurch was very important to her at the last and the padre from the church gave her great comfort."

"Well, I'm sorry I can't be of more help," replied the administrator haughtily. "Perhaps if you sent an email to us giving all the details of why you want to go in and your connection with the church. And how long you would need to be inside. Oh, and you would need to guarantee that any photographs or videos you took there would be for your own personal use and not uploaded to social media or used in some other way. Frankly, as you may know, the place may be pulled down soon, and we have our own legal arrangements with the developer to think about." And, with that, she indicated that the interview was over and escorted Roderick briskly across the yard to the gate.

Roderick Scott walked out into the street. He was flustered and very upset. He nearly got run down by a large red London bus in his confusion forgetting to look the correct way when crossing the busy thoroughfare. He could understand now what his wife had been writing about. To think that the lovely old padre had been swamped with this level of central bureaucracy and control.

However, had the man kept his temper and continued to preach the Christian faith? In Arkansas, if some officious, snobbish head office type had behaved in this fashion. Well, I'm not in Arkansas, I will just leave it at that, he thought.

Once he had crossed safely over to the cathedral on a whim, he bought a copy of the evening newspaper that had the words 'Protest at Cathedral' displayed prominently on its font cover. Pushing through the crowds milling on the cathedral steps, he sat down on one of the wooden benches near the Temple Bar monument and started to read. It was then that he saw a handbill wedged into the seat near him with the words St Mary Abchurch displayed prominently in red upon it. Quite excited by now Roderick leant over and retrieved the leaflet. In it, he read about the proposed sale, about the importance of the church building and about Sir Christopher Wren who of course had also built St Paul's Cathedral itself which rose majestically immediately in front of him.

And here on the front of his newspaper was a picture of that same leaflet. Roderick opened the paper and read about the protest which had taken place only the day before. He saw a picture of two young women holding a banner up high and several policemen escorting them from St Paul's. *So the British do care about their history and architecture*, he thought. *Well, at least some of them do.*

After reading further, he decided to try contacting the ladies to discover the full story behind the leaflet. He was only in London on holiday he told himself, but he was retired, and there were no constraints on his time. Besides he loved a challenge. So picking up the newspaper and leaflet he retraced his steps slowly up Cannon Street until he was once again in Abchurch Yard in front of the Vintry pub.

It was by now late afternoon and the yard was rapidly coming alive with drinkers chatting and laughing as they left the office for the day. As he entered, the square one of his drinking friends from earlier saw him. "Hey, sir, did they give you the keys to get into St Mary Abchurch?" he asked. "Perhaps we could all join you to get inside to have a look."

"No, they didn't. In fact, the person I saw was rather rude to me, and I'm still very cross about it," said Roderick sharply.

"Well, you should come and join our discussion in the pub which is just about to start. You might not know, but there was a demonstration in St Paul's Cathedral yesterday about St Mary Abchurch. It's been in the newspapers and on the television news. And those ladies from the cathedral demonstration are holding a meeting here downstairs in the Vintry to decide what to do next. I believe they are trying to get as many people as possible to join them in signing a petition to save this church. There is even a clergyman down there believe it or not who wants to help us."

"Wonderful!" exclaimed Roderick who was by now very excited indeed. "They can tell me all about this leaflet. I've no time even to think about having a drink. Show me where the meeting is. Lead me to it! My visit to London is turning out to be much more interesting and worthwhile than I ever imagined."

Chapter 9
Covent Garden

Dorothy Normanton bubbled with excitement at the prospect of attending the ballet at the Royal Opera House for the first time. She barely ever ventured from Richmond-on-Thames into central London. In fact, she used to tell friends that she knew continental capital cities far better than she knew her own. This occasion would therefore be doubly memorable for her. The immediate problem was what to wear.

Did the followers of the ballet wear evening dresses, lounge suits or even casual attire? The chairman's secretary assured her that smart casual would be ideal and that the chairman's wife always wore blue, probably a smart blue summery dress on this occasion. So that was sorted, and of course, her husband would never be parted from his clerical collar.

Bishop Leo had also been excited by the prospect of visiting Covent Garden but his evening had been somewhat overshadowed first by the meeting in the Guildhall Old Library but later by the demonstration in St Paul's Cathedral. Both events had received fevered publicity in the domestic media so much so that the Archbishop of Canterbury had telephoned him that very morning to discuss the best way for the Church of England to extricate itself from the difficulty which was now, as the Archbishop saw it, in danger of moving from being a local to a national or even an international issue.

Dorothy sensed the matter was more complicated than her husband was admitting, so she urged him to put it all out of his mind just for one evening. "It's our first time at the ballet," she implored her husband, "and I have been so looking forward to it. Forget that St Mary Abchurch matter for one evening. TPL has been so considerate to invite us."

Bishop Leo sighed, agreed and followed his wife to the waiting car.

At the opera house, the chairman of TPL and his wife were standing waiting in the foyer as Leo and Dorothy arrived. They greeted and kissed their guests, pointed out the cloakroom and happily chatted together as they showed them the newly refurbished foyer.

"Have you seen The Sleeping Beauty before?" asked the chairman politely of Dorothy as he bought theatre programmes and led his guests to their seats on an aisle near the front of the stalls, on his way nodding to various people he knew.

"Well, not actually that particular ballet. I did see Swan Lake when I was a teenager. I've always meant to see it, but it just never happened. Leo is so busy and the months just vanish. You know how it is. As you get older, the years go by more quickly," she whispered, verbose in her awkwardness. "But I've looked up the story on the internet, so I'm quite prepared. Isn't this theatre grand, all this red and gold? I like the little lights around the balconies."

The chairman swallowed hard and said, "TPL has sponsored Covent Garden for many years, both ballet and opera, and we always have these same four seats, near the aisle. Easy to slip in and out. I seem to do a lot of corporate entertaining these days. If you decide you like the ballet we must come again together."

By now, the theatre was quickly filling up. The four sat down and began to read their glossy red programmes. At least the chairman and his wife did. Leo and Dorothy were absorbed in turning around to watch other patrons as the opera house buzzed with excitement. "Look there," said Bishop Leo pointing excitedly and squeezing Dorothy's arm, "it's that man from the BBC, or is it commercial television. You know who does the food shows," he added helpfully.

"Oh no," Dorothy saw where he was pointing and corrected him apologetically, "unless people are in the Church of England you have no idea about celebrities. He's a BBC weatherman. I saw him putting his coat in the cloakroom when we arrived. He was talking to a rather attractive very young lady. I'm sure it's not his wife."

"Oh yes," agreed Bishop Leo crestfallen. "My goodness, a packed house tonight. This should be a good show."

The house lights slowly dimmed, and the conductor arrived to great applause and indicated to the musicians to take a bow.

"Surely we shouldn't clap before the performance," said Dorothy. Leo didn't reply.

The music began. Dorothy, still trying to look at the weatherman, in the darkness inadvertently dropped her programme onto the floor.

"Leo please get it for me. I need my programme," she said loudly. A man behind said 'shush!' also very loudly. "Well, the actual dancing hasn't started yet," she muttered to herself indignantly, "it's just the opening music." The four then settled back for what they hoped would be a relaxing evening.

As Dorothy explained later whilst they were being driven home, with lovely music playing in a theatre that was both warm and dark, she inevitably felt tired. What did they expect? She had had a long day with so much to remember, and she had to make sure that she was dressed ready, for when the car arrived. And, anyway, why was the temperature in those places kept so high? And she was certain that she did notice when the dancers appeared because she thought she recognised one of them from a TV advert for dog food. Although to be truthful the thing, she definitely remembered was her husband poking her in the side.

"You are falling asleep my dear. Don't upset our hosts and do keep your mouth closed," he whispered.

"I'm not asleep," she said indignantly.

"Well, someone was snoring, and it wasn't me," said her husband.

By now, the man behind had had enough.

"Look," he said leaning over, "these seats are expensive enough without having to listen to you two."

"Well, I might have nodded off for a second or two," she whispered to Leo, "but at least I'm not like that man on the other side of me who keeps pretending to conduct the orchestra. Why ever must he do that!"

The first interval arrived and the chairman and his wife, smiling but with obvious inner relief, led their guests to a table in the Floral Hall set with champagne and canapés.

"Are you both enjoying it?" the chairman asked. "Does it meet your expectations?"

"Oh yes, it's magnificent," said Bishop Leo. "And such good seats. You are spoiling us both. For me, although the dancing is good, I often think the music is the best part."

"Well, there are two intervals in Sleeping Beauty so please take your time enjoying the champagne. We can have ice cream and coffee later on, and there may be a little time to look inside the theatre shop. Let me check if they keep it open this late."

"I'm surprised you men aren't talking about St Mary Abchurch what with all that's taking place, meetings in the Guildhall Library and riots in St Paul's Cathedral," said the chairman's wife to the obvious irritation of her husband who was indicating to her quite clearly that the subject was not for discussion tonight.

"No, I told you before we arrived, that's business, and we are all having an evening off," he replied crossly.

The bishop agreed, "It is a bit harsh to call it a riot. Just a small difference of opinion I think, in spite of the calamitous headlines in the daily press. Newspapers always exaggerate as we all know."

A warning bell sounded and then an official from the opera house walked through the dining area ringing an old-fashioned handbell.

"No need to rush," said the chairman. "If you have finished the champagne let's make a leisurely return to our seats. Washrooms are over there," he indicated to Dorothy. "Oh, do excuse me for a moment. I can see one of our major shareholders by the bar. I just need a very quick word. My wife will show you back to our seats."

91

Dorothy and Bishop Leo were enjoying the evening. The opera house really did impress. Dorothy in particular had spotted several celebrities from the radio or television but irritatingly could not remember the names or context for most of them.

She laughed to Leo, "People at places like this should be compelled to have name badges. I like to know who famous people are and see what they are wearing. I feel I want to get a few to sign my programme. I bet they would be flattered to be asked."

"My goodness, my love. You will do no such thing. I would be so embarrassed," he said, relieved to see that she was laughing and joking.

The ballet evening was obviously a great success with the guests, and it was with some reluctance that the bishop and his wife finally gave thanks to their hosts, retrieved their coats and found the car waiting in Bow Street for the journey back to Richmond.

"You know," said Dorothy curling up in the warm seat, "we should have a return match so that we can take them out to a show. Pity the Church of England doesn't sponsor something like the Royal Opera House. All you get as a perk are soaps and shampoo which you pinch from hotel rooms at clergy retreats."

"Yes," said Leo absentmindedly. His mind was starting to wander. Nowadays St Mary Abchurch was never too far away from his thoughts.

"The trouble is I rather suspect that the publicity around this damn St Mary Abchurch business has somewhat upset TPL. I sense they are having second thoughts. That major shareholder he went over to talk to could be significant. I noticed that he looked towards us once or twice, and I felt sure that St Mary Abchurch had been mentioned. I'm starting to wish I had never heard of the place!" he said with feeling.

"And that demonstration at the cathedral the other day came straight after the disrupted meeting at the Old Guildhall Library. I called the dean this morning, and he believes the people at the cathedral are the same ones who walked out of the TPL meeting. Bryan has been doing a bit of research too, and it seems that some of these protesters may have been part of the congregation at St Mary Abchurch before the place was closed down some months ago, even before I took over the diocese I might add."

"Oh, now, I understand." Dorothy was suddenly awake. "You are the new bishop here, and they are trying to sabotage your tenure of office before it has barely started. That's probably at the bottom of all this."

"Maybe," said Leo. "Canterbury is on our side though. The Archbishop called earlier and told me he didn't want to hear the details. He just wanted the matter sorted out as quickly as possible with the minimum of publicity. He indicated that he would fully support what I did as long as it was kept out of the national newspapers and especially away from the television and radio news."

"Well, best of luck with that Leo. Didn't you tell me that a BBC van was parked outside St Paul's?" Dorothy said as she drifted off to sleep.

Chapter 10
The Abchurch Militant
Association

Roderick hurried to join the meeting downstairs at the Vintry.
He introduced himself to Nancy, Karen and Rev John and
gave them a few brief details of why he was interested in St
Mary Abchurch. He told them about his somewhat hostile
reception at the bishop's office and the cavalier way he had
been treated. Rev John apologised and explained that he
worked in the same office although he didn't give much else
away at this stage. He knew that he would have to tell his new
friends about his former dealings with Aubrey and Joan, but
he hadn't decided yet exactly how and when to do this.

Roderick continued, "I am determined to travel to East
Anglia to see Aubrey and Joan before I go home. Some
friends here at the Vintry gave me their address, but if I can
help out with your plans to save this church in the meantime
then I'm very happy to be involved. And look I don't want to
sound like a rich American from over the pond, but I'm very
happy to underwrite any plans within reason that you come
up with to prevent the church's destruction and indeed reopen
it for daily worship. I've spent my business life amongst many

of the well-known financiers on Wall Street in New York, and I'm sure I could arouse serious international financial support for you. It so annoys me when head office functions don't understand what keeps their business alive and who it is that provides the sheer guts of the day-to-day operation."

Nancy, Karen and Rev John were very pleased indeed to have an experienced businessman like Roderick join their nascent campaign and several patrons from the Vintry also joined in with offers of help. That evening this first meeting came up with the idea to set up a national or perhaps an international petition to be signed online by a target of a million people.

"That number is just preposterous and far too large and beyond our abilities," laughed Karen when the figure was agreed upon by those present. "I think we are all becoming over-excited. We might be fighting against the church authorities after all. We have to be sensible and measured."

"No, you are missing the point," roared Roderick standing up and speaking loudly. "We don't have to be measured or sensible. We have to create as much fuss as possible and be a public nuisance, and we have done it now whilst the media is interested. Force the Church of England to take note and listen.

"We have no time to be sensible and measured. The bulldozers will be here soon to knock the place down if I understand you right. Speed and maximum publicity should be our watchwords. Now is not the time to be either sensible or measured."

"Well, it's certainly true that the magistrate this morning appeared to be in support of what we were doing. I've never been to a Magistrate's Court before, but a promise to keep the peace does not seem to be a terrible punishment. I was expecting much worse. And the Church of England wasn't even present in the court," said Nancy.

"I can tell you the Diocese of London just wants the matter to be forgotten as quickly as possible," nodded Rev John.

For the rest of the evening, the Abchurch Militant Association, as they now named themselves, spent time drawing up a simple petition to put on social media, outlining their two aims and their objections to the sale and demolition of St Mary Abchurch. Nancy's husband was an IT specialist for a major insurance group and in his absence he was given the job of organising the technical side of the enterprise.

"Don't worry about him," Nancy had assured the meeting. "He will be only too happy to help out. He loved organising the printing and distribution of those leaflets we handed out in the cathedral."

That same evening, over a few drinks in the basement of the Vintry, the members of the Abchurch Militant Association organised themselves into a focussed campaign. None of them had any experience with such an enterprise, but it was surprising just how much could be achieved by throwing ideas onto the table. Nancy and Karen crafted new leaflets and a suitable logo for Abchurch Militant. Roderick arranged to fund the enterprise and obviously took on the role of treasurer. Rev John appointed himself to oversee the publicity of the campaign with churches throughout England as well as with the media generally. Many drinkers from the Vintry joined in as well, giving their names to assist in the distribution of material and publicity in the suburbs and wider afield.

"I think our next action point should be to go down to Suffolk to see our old vicar and his wife," said Karen. "Let's see if he will add his support to this enterprise. He may even be persuaded to come up here to address a meeting or two especially as he has apparently not been to London for such a long time."

"Excellent idea," agreed Nancy. "Several of the congregation exchanged Christmas cards with Aubrey and Joan last year and many of us had lovely long letters telling us about their new life in the country. But thinking about it, none of us has actually seen the vicar since that awfully sad day when they said goodbye. I'm sure they both would like to see us and would make us very welcome. And anyway it would be good to hear something of rural life."

"Let me join you," said Roderick. "I did intend to meet them on this trip anyway. It should be a great day out. And, on my own, I might get very lost even trying to find how to get to East Anglia."

"Will you come along with us Rev John?" asked Karen.

"No, not at this stage I won't join you. Another time," John brushed off the invitation.

"It's a pity we can't get inside St Mary Abchurch to take a few pictures to take with us to East Anglia. I'm sure Aubrey would get quite emotional if he saw his old church," said Karen.

Rev John looked up. "If you are serious in saying that, I know I can obtain the key," he said furtively. "I would be seriously reprimanded if word of this leaked out though," he added as an afterthought.

Nancy spoke for them all. "Look John it would be special to be able to get inside our old church again, but we wouldn't want you to jeopardise your position in the church if you were found out. Would you be taking a really big risk?"

"Probably," said Rev John, "although if someone saw me I would claim I left something by mistake inside the church when I visited the other week with the TPL officials. The real issue might be if you were all seen entering the building. We have been forbidden to allow access to the general public at the moment. Give me a couple of days to think this through."

Over the next week, the four friends worked rapidly to put some structure into their campaign of opposition. Nancy lived in the inner suburbs of London, and she provided a room where they could meet to plan tactics and store publicity materials. Her husband set up a computer in one corner and established various accounts on different social platforms. Within a week, an official petition had been drawn up and posted online with the exhortation that anyone and everyone could sign it. Money was not being requested as, unusually for such an enterprise, it was being funded entirely by one person, Roderick.

Paper copies of the petition were printed and then distributed by patrons of the Vintry to many pubs and restaurants throughout the London area and even further afield. Rev John sent several to his friends in the Diocese of London, especially to those who had been at the presentation in the Guildhall. And, more significantly, he also sent copies to most sections of the national press based in the capital.

Roderick himself was in touch with various colleagues on Wall Street in New York City asking them to become involved financially, and his local lawyer in Arkansas agreed to set up a tax-efficient organisation called the American Friends of St Mary Abchurch to promote the church and its activities throughout the United States. Leaflets there were rapidly printed headed simply 'Save St Mary Abchurch' and were rapidly distributed throughout North America to many Christian denominations. The campaign suddenly sprang into life and took on a life of its own over there, even amongst people who were not really sure where St Mary Abchurch or indeed the City of London could be. And as the days wore on and after years of rapidly declining religious faith in the United States, Canada and Great Britain it seemed to many that the very idea of this St Mary Abchurch campaign might come to symbolise almost a last attempt of the Christian faith to save itself on both sides of the Atlantic. Later that month, the various petitions easily reached a million signatures and soared very much higher after that. Many thought that the New World was again coming to help out the Old for the betterment of both sides of the Atlantic.

All this endeavour was planned to climax in a large open meeting to which the friends wanted to invite Aubrey and Joan Braithwaite, the last Mr and Mrs Vicar of St Mary Abchurch.

"It would be such a fitting tribute to them," said Karen. "Although I doubt they would be bothered to come along. They must have forgotten the church by now. But we must go to see them just to try to persuade them. They have so many friends here who remember them with such warm affection."

Nancy agreed. "I suspect they might be rather flattered to be consulted. The vicar I seem to remember could easily get emotionally involved in matters to do with his beloved St Mary Abchurch."

Rev John came along one Saturday evening with the key to St Mary Abchurch as he had promised. The four friends quietly let themselves into the church when the Vintry pub was closed for the weekend, and it was very unlikely they would be overlooked.

Stepping back into the church after so many months was a very emotional experience for both Karen and Nancy. When John had locked them all inside, Karen had to sit down, overcome as she was with her many memories and with sheer happiness. She then walked quickly around the building showing Roderick some of its treasures.

"And Aubrey would stand just here," she pointed in her excitement. "He always stood in this spot to shake hands with everyone as they left. And that's where he baptised the bell just before he left for good. Up there is the royal coat of arms. He preached about it once I remember.

"Come over here to the font and let me show you how the heavy cover moves up and down. The mechanism is quite basic, and there is a counterbalancing weight in the vestry near Aubrey's desk," she explained. "And this little seat near the ancient poor box was where the church beadle would sit during Divine Service in Victorian times. Aubrey always maintained that was so. The beadle would keep order at the back of the church and stop unruly children from talking I always imagine."

Roderick smiled and followed Karen further around the building. He put his arm in hers, "I understand your enthusiasm. I can also sense the very Christian ambience in this place. Like Rev John I too feel the presence of the thousands who have passed this way before us," he said.

And then he suddenly stopped. "Please let's all be very quiet just for a moment. Let's listen to the building." All four stood still. "You know," he continued, "I can hear the church praying around us in the silence. St Mary Abchurch is willing to succeed. This place is truly holy ground.

"I'm so pleased to have had the chance to get inside. As you know, my wife died in a street nearby, so she never saw the church from outside or inside, but I think Aubrey was enthused so much about it whilst he was comforting her as they waited for the ambulance that she felt she knew the place. Rev Aubrey sensed what I also felt. He knew the importance of prayer. In a strange way, I feel I knew this place before I ever arrived in London."

Both Karen and Nancy took photos of the church interior from different vantage points on their mobile phones. "I will get a few of the best ones printed up for Aubrey and Joan before we travel down to see them," she said excitedly, "especially this one taken from up in the pulpit. Aubrey doesn't have a mobile phone of course," she laughed, "so it really doesn't matter what angles we take. He won't have seen anything similar."

"Please don't drop any of our posters and leaflets by mistake," warned Rev John. "That would give me away. If you are all ready I think we had better let ourselves out of the church now, so I can quietly return the key to its proper place in my office."

The four friends walked back out into an empty Abchurch Yard. No one spoke. John locked the main door then each, deep in their own thoughts, went home their separate ways.

Chapter 11
Bryan in Charge

The activities of the Abchurch Militant Association and the friendships it provided gave Rev John a renewed Christian vigour. At lunchtime, instead of walking alone in the lanes and squares of the City of London, he could now be found typing vigorously on his iPad at his office desk.

"Whatever is he doing so earnestly?" Bryan eventually quizzed Father Adrian. "He is your colleague. You surely must know what he is up to."

"I don't know what you mean. He does some work on his iPad at lunchtime if that's being 'up to' something as you put it. Probably he's involved in outside charity work I expect. Why don't you ask him," replied Adrian, "I haven't questioned him as it's none of my business."

Bryan snorted and returned to his desk. He knew that something was happening nevertheless. John was just so self-contained and secretive nowadays. He still did his office duties of course but Bryan, ever suspicious, started to suspect that John was involved in things which might be to the detriment of the new bishop. But unlike Rev John and Father Adrian, Bryan just did not have the contacts within the diocese whom he might ask, and more importantly, he did not use social media, so he was oblivious to the expanding efforts of the Abchurch Militant Association or even to its existence.

Then, suddenly, by chance, Bryan was presented with the opportunity to discover more. One Thursday all the office staff left work on time to have a drink in a local tavern, so they could enjoy the warm summer evening together. When the last employee had left the diocesan offices and the rooms were quiet, Bryan quickly walked over and examined Rev John's desk drawers. The secret was out. A small pile of the Abchurch Militant leaflets was lying in the bottom drawer along with a few letters, hidden under John's iPad.

Bryan extracted a leaflet and letters and returned to examine them in his own room. He couldn't believe what he was reading. This gang of troublemakers from the Guildhall and from the cathedral were actually planning more problems for the diocese and probably for the whole Church of England. And there was Rev John's name on the leaflet. So that was what had been happening, organised from right under the nose of Bishop Leo here in his actual office. Were he, Jude and Leo the very last to know what was being plotted in the centre of the London diocese itself?

There was a noise in the outer office. Bryan quickly hid the leaflet as Bishop Leo himself appeared after an afternoon in the House of Lords.

"Oh, hello, Bryan," said the bishop, "you still here. I'm rather cross, after all my work I just didn't get a chance to talk in the debate this afternoon."

"Forget the House of Lords, Bishop. Something I've found out is much more serious for you and for us all," exclaimed Bryan.

He showed the leaflet to Bishop Leo and for the next hour discussed the probable implications of its contents with an increasingly incredulous bishop.

Leo suddenly paused and wiped his forehead, "Bryan, some matters are starting to make sense. I think I understand now what some of the other bishops in the Lords were whispering about yesterday. I saw them looking over some leaflets which they hid away suddenly when I approached. They obviously knew about this campaign to stop TPL and didn't want to embarrass me.

"It seems I was the only person who was kept in the dark and the worst aspect is that it is all taking place in my see, the Diocese of London. I wonder if the Archbishop has picked up on their campaign. Perhaps he hasn't yet as he would probably have called me if he had read this leaflet. However, can I stop all this, Bryan? Is it too late? Has it gone too far to stop?"

"Well, I think it gets worse, Bishop," said Bryan. "It looks as though Rev John himself has been a leader of all these protests if you can believe it, and he helps plan them right here in the diocesan offices. That's why he works away on his iPad each lunchtime. I shouldn't be surprised if he didn't organise that shameful riot in St Paul's the other week. He is clearly not to be trusted. You have to deal with him, bishop, whilst you still can. Perhaps if you were forceful with him that might at least slow down the campaign."

"Mind you," Bryan continued pensively, "I suspect it might be difficult at this stage. I forgot to mention that I saw a letter from New York on John's desk. American money and friends are being brought into the equation. That might mean serious trouble for us."

Bishop Leo groaned and sat with his head in his hands. "I don't know what to say. I know I have had to be away a lot in the House of Lords on important matters just recently, but I did rather expect that you and Jude would keep things under control back here. Whatever will I say to the chairman of TPL? I often bump into him in parliament.

"He took Dorothy and me to the ballet at Covent Garden only the other week, and this is how I repay him. Sabotaging his project. That's what he will think. What else could he think? It's just not good enough, really Bryan. The Archbishop of Canterbury will certainly become agitated if the press and television take an interest in all this.

"Nothing upsets Lambeth Palace and the Archbishop's staff more than stories appearing in newspapers over which they have no control. It will all reflect rather badly on me. I was promoted to this senior bishopric in the belief that I was a safe pair of hands. I could keep the ship steady as they say. If I fail in this appointment then I, and that includes you and Jude remember, will progress no further." His voice at first soft was now quite strident and becoming ever louder.

"And," said Bryan warming to the conversation, "it seems not only do this group of troublemakers want to destroy the TPL arrangement, the very deal which Rev John himself has been heavily involved with in the past by the way, but they want to reopen St Mary Abchurch as a parish church, and just look at the wording at the bottom of the leaflet, their second prominent aim is to restore the Book of Common Prayer and the King James Bible there and elsewhere in the Church of England."

"Yes, I read that, and it really makes me very very cross," fumed Bishop Leo. "Both Rev John and Father Adrian know that one of my missions in life is to stamp out that old nonsense, especially Cranmer's prayer book. We aren't in the Middle Ages. We are driving young people away from the church by using old-fashioned words and phrases and suchlike. Haven't you explained that to them, Bryan? The church needs young people or it will die and the young will not have ancient prayer books which they do not understand! I'm sure I'm right. You understand what I am saying, don't you, I hope?"

"Of course, you are right bishop, and I have repeated this many times to both John and Adrian. Frequently in fact," said Bryan smiling smugly. And he continued, "I sense all this is just an indication that the diocese we inherited has allowed itself to become too disorganised. There is no serious office structure. It's an issue we must have a longer chat about sometime.

"I've a few ideas for changes. I blame the previous bishop. By the way, ironically, I had been told that Rev John very much agreed with you over the issue of the Book of Common Prayer. He has clearly changed his mind. I can't imagine why he would do that."

Bryan sat down in front of the bishop's desk. "The question for you Leo is what we are going to do about it. I think social media may be picking up on their campaign, and it is clear that interested parties across the Atlantic are also watching. I will ask Jude to trawl various internet sites to keep us up to date. I might caution that we need to move quickly before the *London Press* starts to take a serious interest in this so-called campaign.

"Much of what happens in the United States becomes almost domestic news in England these days. On a personal matter, of course, we could just lose Rev John elsewhere in the diocese, rather as we did before in your last clerical post with that other self-opinionated young man as I'm sure you will remember. Although on reflection I'm not confident that such a move would stop the trouble-making this time."

The bishop was no longer listening. He was deep in thought, a worried frown on his face.

He said, "I know I can trust you, Bryan. Let me let you into a little secret. Since I became bishop here, in just a short few weeks I have seen into a whole new world. I am often in the House of Lords as you know. I chat to the Archbishop of Canterbury now rather as an old friend, and I feel he seeks out my opinions on many subjects, and between ourselves, Bryan one or two hints have already come my way that I may move even higher in the church hierarchy one day.

"Even my wife senses that. And, in fact, it was Dorothy who first suggested to me the idea that these demonstrations might be personal in nature and were being planned to destroy my career in the diocese and the wider church. I wasn't so sure but seeing that leaflet makes me think she may be right. As we both know, enemies are made in the church, as they are in any large organisation."

Leo stood up and began walking determinedly up and down his office.

"This TPL project Bryan, even though I didn't invent it, has become so important for me and my time in this bishopric as through it I expect to stamp new ideas on a major City of London development and as the Archbishop himself told me only last week I personally will always be associated with it in the public mind. Oh, and of course, it will free up desperately needed funds for our mission work here," he added as an afterthought.

Bryan smiled and nodded in agreement.

The bishop continued crossly. "Just look at some of the statements made in this leaflet. It talks about saving St Mary Abchurch, no, even more than that. From its language, the implication is that we should expand and even reopen redundant parish churches. It really does exasperate me, Bryan.

"It goes against all recent experience. The City of London has far too many churches, you yourself have often told me that. And as for Rev John," he hesitated, "when he comes in tomorrow tell him to come and see me. I will consider what I am going to say to him later tonight. I will discuss the matter with my wife. Dorothy always has good suggestions.

"No, on reflection, not tomorrow the parliamentary debate on the future of the railways is still going on, and I'm prepared to speak in it. Make it the day after. I will see him first thing on Thursday. My time is so busy. I have the synod meeting next week then I'm due to chair a meeting on safeguarding and all this needs to be woven into my parliamentary duties. Perhaps after Rev John has seen me I might ask you to deal with the situation. Leave the leaflet here."

The following day, Bryan was waiting when John arrived for work.

"The bishop needs to see you urgently first thing tomorrow morning. Get a slot in his diary for nine o'clock at the latest. I don't know the details," he dissembled, "although he talks about some leaflet he has come across."

For the rest of the morning, Bryan could be heard whistling and singing as he walked around the office. He had a coffee with Jude, mentioned the leaflet and asked him to look over the various social media sites to see if the campaign had been mentioned. At lunchtime, he interviewed a young prospective minister for one of the smaller churches on the north side of the city.

"I hope you will fit easily and loyally into the City of London," he spoke plainly and loudly. "We are removing the pews from the church before you take over and replacing the old prayer books with modern service pamphlets. I hope neither will be a problem for you."

The new minister smiled and nodded in agreement. "I will use whatever suits you and Bishop Leo," he said, "I'm just so grateful to be spending part of my career in the Diocese of London."

At the mention of Leo, Bryan frowned. "Actually, there is no need for you to see the bishop personally. He is just so busy right at the moment. But I'm his right-hand man, the bishop, and I think as one. I will let him know that we have agreed on the way forward. But let me reiterate, Bishop Leo does value loyalty from his staff before anything else, as you would expect of course." His voice boomed the word 'loyalty' around the office.

The new vicar continued to smile and assured Bryan that he would do whatever was required. He was so very pleased to be given this chance in the Diocese of London. He then consulted his prepared notes and started to explain some of his plans for his new church.

"I thought I might distribute a few service brochures to local businesses and start an evening prayer session one day a week after work," he explained enthusiastically.

Bryan stopped him impatiently. "Yes, yes, all of that. Well, we are very busy here in the diocesan office. I will pop by to see how you have settled down sometime in the next few months."

And indicating the meeting was over he shepherded the new vicar to the door. "Good to have you in the city. I will see if the bishop, or failing him me or my colleague might take a Communion Service at your new church when you and your wife have settled in." The new vicar beamed and vanished quickly into the street.

Whilst Bryan was walking back to his desk, Jude rushed over to see him.

"My goodness, Bryan. Various parts of social media are alive with a campaign to stop our rebuilding project with TPL. Come over and look at my computer."

Bryan put his finger to his lips. "Quiet, Jude. Just between the two of us."

"Well," continued Jude excitedly, "there is a long stream of people signing a petition to stop our proposed rebuilding arrangement with TPL and instead reopen St Mary Abchurch, rewire and relight it and generally clean it up as 'a Christian beacon fit for the twenty-first century' as one incumbent from somewhere in the East Midlands has written."

Bryan groaned. "What nonsense! But just as I feared and in fact as I told Leo last night, we probably can't stop this now. Please read all the daily newspaper clippings and listen to radio and television over the next few days. Give me a daily morning briefing, so we can at least keep the bishop informed. Then, the three of us will have to make a decision on how to proceed."

Rev John arrived early for work on Thursday morning. He had spoken to his colleagues of course as he realised he would now have to justify his actions.

Nancy and Karen had been particularly worried and had tried to reassure him.

"It's kind of you," Rev John had smiled, "but I knew what I was doing. I'm not blaming anyone. I thought it all out beforehand. I knew this day would come. It's in my stars! It's just that it's all happened rather quickly.

"The bishop will put a stop to any career I might have hoped for in the Church of England. He's become a powerful man, and he's well in with the Archbishop of Canterbury's staff apparently. Leo is a person who has firm favourites, and I have never felt that I fit in. When he arrived here with Bryan and Jude, two colleagues from his previous work, I sensed I had been demoted, to be honest. Although, on a personal level, he doesn't really have much to do with my day-to-day work as he is usually away on his House of Lords business."

"Well, will you change your mind and come to Suffolk with us to see Aubrey and Joan?" Karen had asked, trying to change the subject.

"Probably not. The couple, well Aubrey at least, will undoubtedly remember me and won't be in any mood to forgive me," he replied sadly. "I told you Rev Braithwaite, and I have had difficult conversations in the past. If you persuade him to come up to the city for our meeting then I will try to make my peace with him then."

Bishop Leo also arrived early on Thursday and indicated that he wanted a private word with John, 'with the door closed' he said ominously.

"Look at this," thundered Leo holding up the leaflet, "I've discovered from this pamphlet that there is a campaign underway to stop our sale of St Mary Abchurch. The very enterprise which you helped begin, I would remind you. You have not had the courtesy even to speak to me about it, and your name is prominent on the sheet. I'm willing to give you the time to explain yourself properly, although I have to say I'm appalled that you should put your name to any such campaign. Even on my first day here I seem to remember you showed me a mountain of files on this very subject which were stored by your desk. The least I expect from my staff is a certain loyalty to the work of this diocese."

Rev John started to speak but Leo put up his hand and continued, "You have placed me in a difficult position with the chairman of a major property group, a man who is a close personal friend of both me and my wife. And you have brought the attention of the media to this diocese in an unfortunate way. I had hopes that your career might progress to higher roles in the Church of England but now I'm just not sure.

"The first part of any job is to be loyal, both to the institution and to your boss. This leaflet is not loyal. I showed it to my wife last night, and she was appalled. She is usually an incisive judge of people and situations, and she thought it both disloyal and in fact puerile."

There was a knock on the door and the bishop's secretary came in.

"Just to remind you, Bishop, about the meeting at Lambeth Palace with the Archbishop of Canterbury before the later extended debate in the House of Lords. Your car is outside," she said.

"Oh, yes, of course, thank you," said Leo.

Then, continuing to Rev John, "Please give some thought as to how you see your career progressing after this development. Speaking for myself I don't really see you as a long-term fixture in my office. I think it's rather overstaffed anyway. We need to talk in detail again soon. I'm assuming that you won't change your mind about all this and apologise to me and your colleagues here.

"Matters have developed too far I suppose. Oh, and thinking over matters I am in a somewhat busy and difficult period with my parliamentary and other administrative duties at the moment, so I will ask Bryan to interview you to discuss your personal future. He can give me his recommendations later. Now, I must leave."

And Bishop Leo picked up his briefcase and swept majestically out of the office into his waiting car.

Rev John returned dejectedly to his desk and took out an old copy of the Book of Common Prayer. His hands were shaking. He felt himself perspiring. The open-plan office was unusually quiet. The secretaries were avoiding eye contact with him and even his friend Father Adrian appeared to be deeply concentrating on his work. Bryan, however, looked up and smirked condescendingly, "Rev John when you are ready shall we have a little chat at my desk?"

John ignored him, announced to the office generally that he was taking the rest of the day as a holiday, walked out of the building and slammed the front door hard.

"So, after all my work, it has come to this," he thought, "reprimanded like a schoolboy. Whatever could Bryan possibly say to make me feel better even in the unlikely event that he wanted to."

Clutching the prayer book, he walked quickly through the back lanes of the city, keeping close to Upper Thames Street, a main thoroughfare in that part of London, past the lonely tower which is all that remains of St Mary Somerset, until at last, he found the church of St James Garlickhythe, the very church which had been the headquarters of the prayer book Society for many years past. He guessed the churchwardens there would fight to stop the bishop from abolishing the Book of Common Prayer at least in their building. And Leo probably knew that he would have to address the church of St James the very last of all.

He entered the empty building, knelt down to pray and then sat at the end of one of the back pews and opened his prayer book, determined to read and understand as much as possible of the services and exhortations contained there. He turned to the 39 Articles near the back which he had often ridiculed in the past but which he knew were the central elements of the Anglican faith. He had to memorise them years ago at clerical college and as he sat in St James and read through each one he was secretly pleased to realise just how much of his clerical training he remembered. That was a start but to fulfil the second part of his agreement with Nancy and Karen he needed to be familiar at the very least with the basic services of Thomas Cranmer's Book of Common Prayer.

Chapter 12
Aubrey and Joan Braithwaite

At the end of June, Roderick, Karen and Nancy met up as planned at Liverpool Street Station to travel to Suffolk. In spite of their obvious enthusiasm for the journey and their excitement in its arrangement, all were now rather nervous. What specifically would they say to Mr and Mrs Vicar? They had never seen Aubrey and Joan away from the context of St Mary Abchurch and the City of London. They had never even visited their previous vicarage in London.

For Nancy and Karen especially, the vicar and his wife were only as much a part of the city as the church building itself. Perhaps today would be disappointing, a let-down. Perhaps Aubrey would even encourage them to let Abchurch die. In the months since he had left St Mary Abchurch, he had acquired an almost saint-like quality for many of the former congregation. Perhaps those who used to attend services there remembered the situation around the old church somewhat incorrectly. Memory often plays tricks as they all knew.

Roderick for his part had been swept along by the enthusiasm of the others as he sat drinking with them in the Vintry and now he too suddenly wasn't sure how he would be received. Perhaps Mr and Mrs Vicar just didn't want to be disturbed in their country retirement. Perhaps they didn't want to be reminded of their incumbency at St Mary Abchurch. All three were therefore nervous and very quiet for the actual train journey to Suffolk.

The train pulled into Stowmarket on time and the three friends got out, walked along the platform and looked anxiously for Aubrey and Joan. And suddenly there they were. Mr and Mrs Vicar, standing by the exit barrier, had enormous smiles on their faces. All anxiety evaporated in that one moment. Here were the same welcoming people they remembered.

Nancy and Karen in particular felt they were suddenly back at St Mary Abchurch for midday Holy Communion. Time had not moved. There was no need to be anxious. Joan and Aubrey hugged the visitors, including even Roderick whom they had never actually seen until that moment. The small party had a mass of smiles and chatter and then walked out to the vicar's car, and Aubrey hugged the three of them again. His face was one of pure joy.

"As you know, we don't live in Stowmarket but rather in a small village a few miles away. A local rector entrusted me with the job of reopening our small village church. So it's almost been St Mary Abchurch on repeat. Anyway, you will get the full tour a little later," Aubrey said as he started the engine.

"It must be odd working in a village, coming immediately on top of the busy City of London," Nancy remarked.

"Yes, it really is." It was Joan's voice this time. "I have never really lived in such a small hamlet. I grew up in a large market city where my father was dean of the cathedral. Now most of the time, I have to plan each day well in advance.

"I can't just pop out for small items in a local shop for example. Anyway, eventually, we adjusted ourselves. And odd as it probably sounds I couldn't really imagine living in a city again certainly not one as enormous as London."

Aubrey laughed and nodded his head in agreement. "Even I am starting to think that way," he laughed.

The happy party eventually reached their destination. Aubrey parked the car and escorted them to their new home, a very old cottage on the edge of the village.

Roderick laughed, "My goodness Joan this is just lovely. It's the sort of place we Americans think all Brits live in. How old is it?"

"Well, Aubrey has been doing a bit of research in the county library, and I think the oldest section is probably the eighteenth century. So much has been added at different angles over the years as you can see from the outside. We both fell in love with it as soon as we came here. In fact, it was only our first day of house hunting. And it is close to the little church which is just a short walk over the green. Perfect for us both."

The party sauntered up the long garden path admiring the various colourful displays of summer flowers as they went. "I'm the gardener," said Joan, "Aubrey barely remembers the names of garden plants." Inside she had prepared a delicious lunch washed down with apple cider. During the meal, Nancy and Karen told their hosts all about the recent problems with St Mary Abchurch and something of the plans put together between the diocese and TPL.

"Well, actually, we did hear a few rumours of your demonstration in the City of London," interrupted Joan. "Quite surprisingly our small local paper picked up on the St

Paul's rumpus. It didn't have too many details, however, and I certainly didn't know that you two were at the centre of it all," she laughed.

"Good for you."

"Now," she continued, "I'm conscious that your time here is short so let me show you over our home, of which as you can probably tell we are both rather proud, then Aubrey will take you over to see the church. If all that sounds satisfactory we can chat as we walk."

"Just perfect," said Roderick, "but we do need to ask you both some questions about St Mary Abchurch and perhaps ask a favour or two."

He grinned sheepishly. "Don't let us forget."

After Joan had done her tour of their old cottage, Aubrey escorted his visitors across the green towards the church. On entering the grounds, they ran into a retired parishioner who had chosen this day to do his share of cutting back the weeds around the various gravestones. He warmly welcomed Aubrey who introduced him to his guests.

"Oh, you are from London are you, and that Abchurch place. We have heard so much about it. Well, you lost Aubrey and Joan, but we are so happy to have found them. The pair have changed this village in so many good ways. They've opened up the old church, and we get so many people here to Matins on Sunday, a few of them I know for a fact had never been into a church until Aubrey appeared.

"And it is a real treat to hear hymn singing again on Sunday in our village. Did you know we call Aubrey the 'and finally vicar'? Everyone calls him that, even the landlord in the Fox and Crown pub."

"I've never heard that expression," laughed Karen. "May I ask why?"

Aubrey overhearing smirked. "Oh, come on, I can perhaps tell you later if you remind me."

He then showed the three around his small village church.

"We are very proud of this place although, honestly, it is not as well-endowed as many of its larger neighbours in villages roundabout. The proceeds of the medieval wool trade didn't trickle down to this spot. Our main item of interest is this one large medieval tomb with a knight and his lady stretched out on top. We don't even have brasses to rub or significant stained glass windows. Although the pews are old box pews, so I suppose they're important.

"Even though the place is not in the same ecclesiastical league as St Mary Abchurch it has been such fun to reopen and clean it. And we do get a few visitors even from abroad on warm days. You know me with my emphasis on the Book of Common Prayer and King James Bible. Well, we found old copies of each stored in the church tower so from day one all services have used them. I always find the traditional words very much a bridge to all people who have worshipped in the church in the past.

"Rather embarrassingly word of this quickly spread to neighbouring villages with the result that we get many people coming here to Matins and Evensong on Sunday from other parishes. It doesn't necessarily make me popular with some of the local clergy though," Aubrey grimaced, "but I'm too old to change."

He continued, "And, before you ask, we do have a bell. Just the one. Apparently, it can be used after we have replaced the bell pull. It's my mission for next year."

"Now then," said Karen as they walked down the aisle in the centre of the small church past the tomb of the medieval knight and his lady, "What's all this about 'and finally vicar'. We aren't going to let you get away without telling us."

Aubrey laughed out loud, "Well, I'm afraid it's true as George out there told you. That expression has stuck with me. I can't shake it off. Joan you see never comes to Sunday morning matins, which of course usually finishes sometime after midday. Right through our married life, she has never been what I might call, 'a matins person'.

"In the deanery where she was brought up, her father the dean used to refer disparagingly to the wealthy parishioners who came to that service as 'all mink and matins'. Now, she says she can't do matins and a midday meal. But to continue, she is always very strict about meals. Lunch is always on the table sometime around midday. Well, I can hardly run the services precisely to fit in with her cooking.

"As you know, lessons and prayers vary in length, and then, inevitably, I want to chat with the various parishioners. Joan and I had serious words about the issue when we first opened the church. And I occasionally had to eat a cold or tepid meal which she had served up before I got home. The problem was quickly solved, however, when she realised that, as the church has a large, plain glass west window, I could easily see our cottage when I was preaching a sermon standing high up in the pulpit. So she got into the habit of walking down our front path before serving lunch and when she reached the gate she would wave her white pinafore which she knows I can see in the distance whilst I'm preaching."

"I'm listening," said Karen with a puzzled expression on her face, stopping to lean on a pew. "Well, actually, all three of us are paying attention," roared Roderick.

Aubrey continued sheepishly. "Well, when she waves the white pinafore I know a hot lunch will be on the table in ten minutes exactly. Joan is always precise, ten minutes is ten minutes or my lunch will go cold. Well, as I said, I find it difficult to time the services and especially sermons to the minute, so I have to admit that when I see the pinafore flapping in the distance, I do usually say 'and finally' to bring my matins sermon to a close."

"But what if you have only just started the sermon?" questioned Karen.

"Well, that's the point. I tend to say 'and finally' wherever I am in the sermon. I just end whatever I am saying." Aubrey's face started to turn red. "The villagers have quickly seen through me I'm afraid.

"And they all nudge each other and some laugh out loud. In fact, I think a few of the younger members of the congregation come to matins principally to hear me say it. They all know that Joan is waving her pinafore whatever the weather."

The friends all burst out laughing. Nancy linked her arm to Aubrey's. "So no more cold lunches I guess dear vicar."

"Yes," agreed Aubrey sheepishly, "peace was restored in the Braithwaite household. But now virtually everyone calls me their 'and finally vicar'."

They finished the tour of the little village church, said their goodbyes to George as he continued mowing the tall grass growing between the ancient headstones and walked slowly out of the churchyard, then across the village green in the warm afternoon sunlight.

Back in the cottage, Karen took charge as Joan served tea to them all.

"Look vicar," she said, "we wanted to spend a day with you mainly of course to see you and Joan after all these months, but we also need to get some serious advice from you."

Over the next half an hour, the friends described the protests associated with the possible demolition of St Mary Abchurch, the support from the drinkers in the Vintry as well as the media interest in their protest. Nancy and Karen gave Aubrey the photos they had recently taken inside the church. Roderick recounted his shock at seeing the rundown appearance of the church and the discourteous way he felt he had been treated by a diocesan official. And, on top of all this Karen explained, "We are told that our new bishop hates the Book of Common Prayer and the King James Bible."

Aubrey and Joan had kept glancing at each other as the story unfolded before them. Roderick's reminiscence about the diocesan office drew a particularly meaningful smile between the two.

"Our question today vicar is, 'Should we fight to stop this demolition of our church?' No, I don't mean our church I mean your church, or do we just abandon the whole enterprise and worship elsewhere? After all, as we know, there are many churches in London. St Mary Abchurch was closed immediately on your departure, and Nancy and I have had to find another church anyway."

"Although, actually, I'm not sure we will be able to worship long-term elsewhere in the city itself," Nancy butted in. "Our story gets worse. We now have been told that the new bishop not only hates the prayer book, but he is actively trying to get rid of all prayer book services in the diocese. He calls incumbents who use the prayer book, CO priests; apparently, we learn that stands for Cranmer Obsessed."

Aubrey had been very quiet whilst this story was being told. At one point, he looked as though he was about to cry. At last, he leant forward, put his teacup down and spoke softly.

"I sometimes wish I were a much younger man and had the stamina for a real fight with these head office types. But, at my age, it's probably all beyond me and my dear wife."

He gazed around the room at his enthusiastic loving friends, friends who showed their support for him in their excited faces. Suddenly, he sat up straight.

"You know, I'm talking nonsense. I can be involved even though I'm well past retirement age. Why not indeed? Thomas Cranmer was an old man when he was burnt at the stake in Oxford for the Book of Common Prayer.

"So we can at the very least fight to save his work and encourage young people to read and appreciate it. And as for Sir Christopher Wren. Words can't do justice to my thoughts. Surely, in the England of the twenty-first century, we don't have to make the case to preserve buildings constructed by that genius. Yes, of course, I'm with you. Tell me what I can do to help?"

"What can we do to help?" Joan interrupted. "You are not excluding me from this fight." And she squeezed Aubrey's hand.

"Excellent," beamed Karen. "We were secretly hoping for that sort of reaction. Well, next week, we are planning an open meeting officially to launch our campaign to save St Mary Abchurch and at the same time assuming we are successful and it is saved, to bring in a minister trained in the traditional way, as you were vicar, to run it. I think you may be able to help us with some ideas in this area later.

"But perhaps we might persuade you both to come up one more time to the City of London. You would, so help our movement to become instantly popular. And you could give us so much advice on all aspects of the campaign. I'm sure Nancy or I could put you up for the night," said Karen as a final thought to help Mr and Mrs Vicar make the journey.

Aubrey laughed. "Don't worry, I don't really need persuading. As you can see, I'm ready for the fight. I feel new blood already pumping through my veins. I rather suspected you had something planned like this.

"I just wanted to see how committed you all were. By the way, I must tell you that my dear Joan didn't think there could be a role for me at my age," he laughed. "But I told her that if as the prayer book tells us there can be baptism, to quote 'to such as are of Riper Years' then a vicar of 'riper years' should be able to play a role in all aspects of saving the heart and soul of the Church of England. Now, I see time is moving quickly, and I need to get you all back to Stowmarket for the evening train to Liverpool Street."

The day had been a great success. The three friends were tired now, but they still talked excitedly about their plans as the train purred towards London. Having Aubrey and Joan, Mr and Mrs Vicar, involved would be such a great addition to their campaign. So many people in that part of the City of London would remember them. They might even become the living Christian examples of what their fight was all about.

Chapter 13
Mr and Mrs Vicar Return

The day following the journey to Suffolk Roderick Scott decided to find accommodation for a wider meeting of everyone who might wish to be involved in saving St Mary Abchurch.

"Why not meet in the actual church itself," said Nancy.

"That's a brilliant idea," mused John, "but it wouldn't be possible I'm afraid. The diocese would refuse point blank any request from me anyway and if one of you asked they would bombard you with objections. They have already tried to discourage Roderick by quoting Health and Safety issues I seem to remember. The building is very much off-limits for any meeting I think. It's a shame, I agree, as it's the obvious place to attract the general public."

"I looked online," interrupted Roderick, "and I see a few of the livery companies and local schools let out small meeting rooms. Let me try and fix one up for a meeting this weekend."

"Look," Karen exclaimed, "the Vintry offered us that room downstairs free of charge. That will do. I can ask Aubrey and Joan to come up to the city next week and attend the presentation and perhaps make a small speech. It will give them the chance to see the current state of St Mary Abchurch at least from the outside."

An official meeting to launch the campaign to save St Mary Abchurch was therefore arranged to be held in the Vintry in the early evening a few days later, at a time when City commuters would be leaving the various offices dotted in the streets around. Aubrey and Joan as good as their promise made their way to the pub in good time. There they became quite emotional and overcome by the reception they received.

They had approached Abchurch's yard with some sadness. That area of London was after all so tied up with the recent past of both Mr and Mrs Vicar. Walking from Liverpool Street Station they both had become quiet, lost in their own thoughts until they turned down King William Street and into the yard and saw with horror just what had been allowed to happen to St Mary Abchurch. The vast wooden awning still draped the building and although leaflets now covered the yellow graffiti the entire scene was one of neglect and dereliction. The scene in front of them made Joan very cross indeed.

"They have allowed this to happen on purpose," she ventured. "Then, the diocese can say it is just not worth saving. An old trick that. My father would say the same about some old building that stood in the way of a modern development being put together by the deanery."

"Don't get emotional," she said to Aubrey, seeing his look of despair. "I'm sure that inside it is all as we left it, even though we can't get beyond the front door to look at it properly on this visit. Remember, Roderick has rich friends in New York apparently, and they want to improve the church

126

for us. Money can sort this mess. Think about that first day we came here, many months ago.

"Opening up the place and getting it working again seemed an impossible task. But we did it, my love. We did it once, and God willing I'm sure we will repeat the exercise, only this time our numerous friends will not just let it die." And she put her arm through his and kissed him.

Once they had entered the Vintry, their reception was noisy and boisterous. A crowd of several dozen had gathered downstairs. Regular drinkers from the Vintry, parishioners from the various services which Aubrey had led at St Mary Abchurch as well as a few newspaper columnists were all cheering and clapping wildly. The pub landlord had provided three bottles of vintage Spanish cream sherry for the occasion, much to Joan's embarrassment.

"Did we use to drink that much," she smiled going very red in the face. Everyone wanted to ask what life was like in deepest Suffolk.

"I hope your new country parishioners realise that you are only on temporary loan from St Mary Abchurch in the City of London," yelled one drinker to a sustained round of clapping. Aubrey was quite overwhelmed by the scene.

At that moment, Bob, the former organist from Abchurch, appeared laughing and holding a large bunch of summer flowers. "A real vicar," he shouted and rushed to hug both Aubrey and Joan. "I heard a rumour that you would both be here, and I just couldn't miss the occasion."

"Oh, Bob, how great to see you," said Aubrey. "Have you ever thought about living in Suffolk? We really need your services." Everyone in the room laughed and clapped.

Aubrey and Joan were given places at a top table set up at the front of the room, then when everyone had enjoyed yet another drink and sat down Karen called the meeting to order.

"My dear colleagues," she said. "It is probably the proudest day of my life to be able to welcome our own Mr and Mrs Vicar back here, well if not actually back to St Mary Abchurch, back very close to it." She corrected herself.

The clapping and cheering continued as before until Karen put up her hands.

"Friends," she said, "before we start, I have an announcement. As you all know, we established an online petition to save our dear church, and we here in England with our new friends in the United States, friends organised by Roderick here, set ourselves a minimum target of at least one million signatures. A big number, but we thought it might be possible." She winked at Roderick.

"Well, I checked online just now, and I'm pleased to tell you that that figure of one million signatures has now sailed through the two million mark and looks indeed like it may go significantly higher."

The clapping and cheering started all over again. Aubrey who wasn't really sure what an online petition meant beamed with pleasure. Nancy now stood up and proceeded to give everyone a history of the Guildhall protest and especially the disrupted Evensong in St Paul's Cathedral.

The evening then spent time discussing how to proceed, how indeed to stop the deal done by the diocese and how to force the church authorities to reopen St Mary Abchurch as a parish church. Two newspapermen promised to mention the campaign on their front pages and said they would arrange for editorials to be written supporting the campaign. Roderick told the gathering at length about the help now being given by the American Friends of St Mary Abchurch and about the money which would be forthcoming from America to clean up the church and the small square in front. He told the gathering about the interest there now was in America for preserving the magnificent dome, the wooden reredos the covered font and the wooden pulpit.

Many Christians in the United States he explained were quickly and crucially very noisily, coming to the aid of their friends in London. The gathering finally agreed therefore that the next step was for a small team to be sent to request a meeting with Bishop Leo to explore ways to save the church and suggest ending the proposed deal with TPL.

Towards the end when the meeting was breaking up, Rev John moved quickly to the front of the room. He had been hiding away nervously at the back up to this point wondering if he would be presented with his opportunity to apologise. Aubrey spotted him at once and stared.

"Dear Rev Aubrey," said John, "can you find it in your heart just to forgive me? I'm such a self-centred silly young man."

"Who's this?" demanded Joan.

Aubrey replied, "Oh, my dear, Rev John is a young man from somewhere in my past. I did wonder if he was the man I knew when I read his name on that petition." And to John, "There really is nothing to forgive. I don't see a man from my past in front of me now. Life is full of challenges and being good friends in the end is all that matters I think."

He held out a hand to Rev John and both men embraced. "As I understand matters told by Nancy and Karen, you must be crucial now to the campaign to save St Mary Abchurch and if I read the petition correctly you also may be working hard to study the Book of Common Prayer." Aubrey winked and both men smiled. Friends at last. "And, next time, the Abchurch group come down to Suffolk I expect to see you with them."

"Yes, I promise I will be there, Aubrey. I promise."

"Oh, Aubrey," continued John, "before I forget, I found your letter near the altar written for the next vicar of St Mary Abchurch. I have to tell you that it affected me deeply. I'm the only person who has seen it. I took it home to read, and in fact, I still have it; I'm sure you remember that you mentioned me in it."

"My goodness that letter," smiled Aubrey. "I had quite put it from my mind. I wrote it over several weeks and repeatedly changed several pages. Joan never saw it. I have moved on from it. It's your turn to forgive me for singling you out in it."

Both men laughed. "Well, I'm sorry I had the effrontery to open it at all. You said it was for the next vicar of St Mary Abchurch," said John.

"Yes, I did. Perhaps I got that right. Funny how things work out," said Aubrey, and he winked.

"Before we all leave, please take an official badge we have adopted for our campaign," interrupted Nancy. "Our treasurer has kindly donated them and as you can see they have a lovely painted image of the church dome. The very dome which we are determined to see preserved and not cut up for display in any modern lifts."

Nancy's comments started the cheering and clapping all over again. The meeting broke up at last and everyone, now wearing shiny new metal badges, poured out into Abchurch

Yard. "Don't fret dear church," said Karen looking over to the wooden awning, "we won't let you perish."

As matters turned out, however, unexpectedly much of the work of the association was being done for it by TPL itself.

Chapter 14
AGM

Thoughtful Properties Ltd prided itself on regularly organising an uneventful annual general meeting, its AGM. The internal company watchwords secretly nurtured by the board for this event were 'bland' and 'boring'. There was to be nothing controversial or out of the ordinary. The AGM was fixed intentionally to be in the midst of similar annual meetings so that it would be lost and submerged in the pack of others held by competitors at the same time of year. The procedure for the day hardly ever varied.

After introductions from the chairman, progress statements and financials from the treasurer and a few questions posed to board members from the floor, many planted beforehand, the meeting would come to a smooth end allowing shareholders to rush quickly to the adjoining rooms to devour the sandwiches, cake, tea and coffee always thoughtfully provided. A few scuffles might start if the sandwiches vanished too soon, but nothing very serious or detrimental to the reputation of the company and certainly nothing which might get into the national press. To be certain of this, TPL always rehearsed the proceedings beforehand at its head office inside a specially constructed inner room, the same space used before the meeting in the Guildhall Old Library, although in truth there was no need for board members to worry. Nothing was left to chance; bit by bit the company had grown turnover, net profit and dividends year by year. The shares were considered blue chip by the stock exchange and shareholder value was high for an organisation of its type, until that is the company decided in a rash move, not properly thought out some would say, to set up a quasi-partnership with the Diocese of London in the Church of England.

TPL saw the Established Church as a rapidly declining entity with very few years left, a view many thought secretly shared by its archbishops and bishops. Barely anyone now attended its services and some of its ministers seemed reluctant to propagate or even believe the Christian message they were supposed to be preaching. Yet, in spite of these disturbing drawbacks, it was still a mammoth organisation with enormous wealth and vast quantities of real estate, land and buildings.

The board looked at this property portfolio of the church with some envy, a locked-in series of assets waiting to be released. And so, many at TPL imagined that this arrangement with the diocese might just be the first of an endless array of similar deals, a brilliant idea with huge upside potential as the financial papers liked to say. TPL was apparently the first major property company to understand this.

However, in the event, the company had moved too quickly, and in recent days this ecclesiastical arrangement had seemed hastily put together and badly thought out. It had propelled TPL into the newspapers and even onto the nightly television news which was not a place the company directors wanted to be. The campaign group now led by Nancy and Karen had become very vocal indeed.

And suddenly many organisations and all types of people decided to investigate both the St Mary Abchurch contract and even more worryingly, TPL itself. The Church of England might be moribund but many interested parties were willing to rush to its defence if they felt it was under attack. This year therefore the Annual General Meeting of Thoughtful Properties Ltd was 'bland' and 'boring' no longer.

The chairman at first had been very enthusiastic about the arrangement with the church. He liked the bishop and found it easy to get along with him. And he had quickly realised that a deal with St Mary Abchurch could be subsumed into an even larger and more profitable plan to transform the whole area of the City of London to the north side of London Bridge. So, on his advice, TPL had been quietly and secretly buying up properties and rental sites in the streets around for several months and its plans envisaged the new Abchurch Tower as the focal architectural point of a modern office and retail park set squarely in this part of the City.

Commuters would flood daily from London Bridge Station across London Bridge to this new development, work in TPL offices, shop in TPL stores and eat and drink in TPL restaurants and pubs. The models presented at the Guildhall Old Library had given a hint of these ideas but without revealing the full plans.

Now, suddenly, many difficulties had appeared and to such an extent that the chairman and the board were spending long evening hours debating whether or not to proceed. They had planned to make the Abchurch Tower central to the total rejuvenation project but now the board was wondering if the area could be redeveloped without even the involvement of St Mary Abchurch at all. The company share price had plummeted after the rumpus in the Guildhall Old Library to such an extent that a statement had to be made to the stock exchange. Furthermore, major shareholders of course had read about the later trouble in St Paul's Cathedral, and their serious questions started pouring into head office, challenging the wisdom of the whole enterprise.

So today at the question and answer session of the annual meeting the proceedings became dominated by a litany of complaints from city institutions and private investors who were angered by TPL's declining share price. Even the promise of sandwiches and cake did not assuage shareholder anger. Representatives from several architectural societies and church bodies were also present, and they repeated many of the points made earlier in the Guildhall Old Library. After fifteen minutes, the chairman was clearly having great difficulty just to control proceedings. At one point, exasperated he hurriedly whispered something to his fellow board members, left the meeting in the hands of the deputy chairman and rushed away to call Bishop Leo.

"Look, bishop, I understand your desire to see this deal go through," he explained on his telephone call, "I just have to tell you that we cannot proceed without further extensive consideration. We cannot be responsible for the destruction of another Wren church. There, I've said it. The board is unanimous. We might possibly have proceeded with our joint plans if the AGM today was in the mood to agree.

"But it clearly isn't. I'm very sorry. The mood here is really quite ugly. I realise that both our institutions have spent serious money and many hours of work getting this far, but I think we have to call a halt. That's all that I want to say at the moment. I thought you should be the first to know. Now, I must get back to the meeting. I will call with fuller details later."

Back in the meeting, the chairman whispered quickly again to his board colleagues then standing up he announced formally that a statement would be made to the stock exchange to the effect that the arrangement with the Church of England could not now go through in its present form. TPL had failed to appreciate just how important St Mary Abchurch was for the City of London as it was designed of course by Sir Christopher Wren.

The company though as a goodwill gesture would still be contributing a significant amount to the Archbishop of Canterbury's inner city appeal. He then sat down, wiped his forehead on his handkerchief and visibly sighed with sheer relief. He knew that TPL's stock price would bounce back and the shareholders present would today enjoy their sandwiches and coffee.

Later, he called Bishop Leo to report more fully on the mood of the AGM. He explained that the board was unanimous in its desire to pause the building of Abchurch Tower.

"I honestly hope bishop that our two organisations can find another project to work upon in the future, one perhaps that is not so highly visible as destroying a major work by Sir Christopher Wren. I had to call a halt Leo. There was little else I could do faced as I was with such financial pressure. We will proceed with some rebuilding at the north end of London Bridge but without basing it around that tower. It's a pity, I agree, and I was indeed very enthusiastic about the plans we discussed so often in the House of Lords.

"Let's have dinner again soon, so I can share a few other smaller ideas which might be of interest to you. And by the way, although it's not strictly any of my business, might I suggest that you confound all your critics by reopening St Mary Abchurch as a functioning parish church? You might say that both parties had listened to the complaints and acted upon them. Just an idea Leo. Very much up to you of course, as it's an ecclesiastical matter. But it might put both our institutions on the right side of history as I hinted previously." The bishop merely grunted in reply.

After a few further personal remarks, the chairman ended the call sank into his armchair and thankfully drank down the rest of his whisky and soda.

Chapter 15
By Law Established

Bishop Leo arrived at work early the next day. He had not slept much. The comments from the chairman of TPL had turned round and round in his mind through the dark hours. How was he going to explain away the collapse of the scheme to the Archbishop and his fellow bishops? He had talked about it so often to many of them. How could he suddenly agree to reopen St Mary Abchurch after all that had happened over the past few weeks?

It would look like a humiliating backdown. More importantly, there was his own position. He was a major bishop after all; perhaps this episode would make him appear weak and indecisive, hardly suitable to be trusted with such a major role.

He didn't have long to wait. Having drunk his first morning coffee he was sitting down to discuss the future with Bryan when an anxious secretary burst into his office.

"I'm sorry to rush in, Bishop," she burst out, "but Lambeth Palace has just been on the phone. The Archbishop needs to see you over there at once. He asks if you can cancel your morning appointments. Well, in truth, his secretary told me to clear your diary. Apparently, he will explain all when you arrive. I've ordered you a taxi, and here's another cup of coffee."

Bishop Leo sat quietly. His head was throbbing now, confused and muddled by the lack of sleep.

"It's that damned St Mary Abchurch business. I wish we had never heard of the place," said Bryan, seeing the worried expression on his face. "They obviously must know that TPL are pulling out of the deal. Perhaps the chairman has phoned the Archbishop to discuss the matter in some detail. Shall I deal with Rev John whilst you are over at Lambeth Palace?"

"Oh, just forget him, Bryan. First things first. We can deal with him on a personal level later. I've got to try and rescue the wreck of my career out of this business. That's my main focus at the moment."

Bishop Leo quickly swallowed his hot coffee, picked up his briefcase and without saying anything else walked pensively out to the waiting taxi.

He was away for what seemed to be a very long time. The morning appeared to drag, getting longer and longer. The office staff in the diocese were anxious and barely able to concentrate on any work. Would Bishop Leo still be secure in his post after recent events? Would the Archbishop discipline him?

There appeared to be no precedent they could refer to. Lunchtime came and went, and still, there was no word. No one rang from Lambeth Palace. It appeared that the Diocese of London was being ostracised.

Then, suddenly in the middle of the afternoon, a taxi pulled up in the yard and Bishop Leo got out, laughing and whistling, and humming extracts from The Sleeping Beauty. The staff stopped working and watched him as he entered.

"Sorry, I've been so long. You all must have been very worried," he announced to the office in general. "I've just come back from an unplanned lunch at home with my wife Dorothy. I never have weekday lunches at home. I should do it more often. Come into my room Bryan and Jude. I've a lot to tell you. Please close the door."

Bryan and Jude rushed over and sat down by his desk.

"Well," said an exasperated Bryan eagerly. "What did the Archbishop have to say? Was TPL mentioned? What is to happen to John?"

"John, John who?" quizzed Leo.

Bryan and Jude looked at each other, puzzled.

"Oh, you mean Rev John. Please forget him you two. He is not important in the great scheme of church matters," said the bishop rubbing his hands. "Now, what I'm going to tell you is in confidence at the moment, so please respect my faith in you. Believe it or not, but as soon as I arrived at Lambeth Palace, I was rushed into a meeting with the Archbishop of Canterbury, and he just came out with it, no pleasantries, no build-up, nothing."

"Came out with what?" asked Bryan.

"He asked me if I would like to take over as Archbishop of York. Even now my head is still swimming with the idea. The Archbishop of York! Can you imagine! I thought I was dreaming, to be honest, as my head was thumping anyway through lack of sleep. Well, I had a long chat with Canterbury, and I reminded him that I had only been in this diocese here for a few weeks. The Archbishop didn't seem concerned about that.

"He wants a loyal supporter in the north of England was all he could say. By the way, I'm late back because after

140

chatting with the Archbishop I rushed over to see my wife with the news. Dorothy of course on a personal matter would be reluctant to leave her friends in Richmond-on-Thames, but she is adamant that I should say yes. She says I would have to spend periods alone on my own in York if all this happens. But she reminded me that this is what we have both worked for.

"Anyway, apparently, York has decided to step down and retire early for unspecified personal reasons. The Archbishop of Canterbury was careful to say the position had to be seen to be competitive and the appointment process completely transparent. I would be one of two names put forward, but he led me to understand that he would give me the nod if I want it.

"Canterbury has been so pleased with my contributions in the House of Lords apparently and for backing him so strongly in synod and other meetings. He sees York and Canterbury being very much in partnership within the Church of England going forward. That has not always been the case as we know. A loyal, safe pair of hands was how the Archbishop of Canterbury put it."

Bishop Leo beamed, "The Archbishop just asked that if I get the position I must wind up my affairs here as neatly and as quickly as possible. He didn't directly refer to the TPL business although he did make it clear the new Bishop of London must inherit a diocese without any issues which might attract the popular press. That I interpreted as code for us quietly to walk away from any dealings over St Mary Abchurch."

Bryan looked crestfallen and somewhat angry at the news. "Well, I'm delighted we shall be leaving the City of London of course. This is a smug, dreadful place! But I'm cross that Rev John and others will avoid censure over their activities. Did you know he walked out of the office when I tried to interview him the other day? Just murmured something about having a half-day holiday."

"Oh, do forget him, Bryan. Let's move on," said Leo. "I can put a bad annual review on his personal file if you would feel vindicated. My mind is now suddenly totally focussed on York as you can imagine. I'm getting quite excited. Can you get me a large wall map of England, which shows the boundaries of the Province of York, and you might find out discretely how many churches are using old-fashioned services."

Later that same afternoon, Rev John, Roderick and Karen asked to see the bishop to present their petition to him. Bryan and Leo decided to interview them together in what quickly developed into a very frosty meeting. They told the bishop of their online petition and their plans for St Mary Abchurch if the TPL proposals could be dropped.

"Well, it's no secret now," said Bishop Leo. "Our deal with TPL will not now go ahead. I suspect the evening paper may have more details. So I suppose you can congratulate yourselves. You have won," he said sarcastically. "It's what you wanted, isn't it?

"It's what your so-called petition was all about! Although as I see things the scheme has collapsed because of decisions taken by TPL not by the Diocese of London, and frankly it has little if anything to do with your association and its so-called activities."

"I'm not sure it's a matter of winning or losing," said Karen, ignoring the rebuke. "It's just a beautiful gem of a building which we felt the city, no I mean the country could ill afford to see demolished."

"Maybe," said Bryan. "Do any of you realise just how many churches there are in the City of London? Anyway, in spite of our wishes here in the diocese, TPL has pulled out."

Roderick spoke up, "The church of St Mary Abchurch appears from the outside to be in a serious state of neglect although I'm led to believe it is structurally sound. Well, now that you have given us this very welcome news, let me tell you that I'm prepared, with my New York financial backers, to pump as much money into it as necessary to modernise the place, rewire, relight, clean and decorate it. There would be no cost at all to the Diocese of London or to the wider Church of England. I would guarantee that legally."

Bishop Leo and Bryan looked at each other in disbelief not sure how to respond.

"Well, you would need a legal faculty from the diocese to do any work on the church and such approvals can take weeks and months to achieve. The Church of England is by law established, and we need to go through every official procedure," said Bryan smugly, "I think you probably do things rather differently in the United States."

"Whatever it takes," said Roderick ignoring the snub. "Our campaign will employ appropriate designers and workmen to make it all happen. We would ensure that the wider Church of England approved all the work and the workmen being used. We would see this as a partnership of our association with the Diocese of London.

"We just needed to be sure that the diocese wouldn't destroy the church and would allow it to be saved and to continue the style of worship as conducted there until recently by the previous minister, Rev Aubrey Braithwaite. But I guess all that is now assured."

The meeting rumbled on in a somewhat tetchy way until all parties agreed that a legal faculty could be sorted out after relevant renovation plans were drawn up.

Later that same day, Rev John had his separate interview with Bryan although the interview is probably the wrong description as John barely spoke. He was harangued by Bryan for twenty minutes. He was effectively blamed for the collapse of the TPL scheme even though he had been the one working on it before Leo became Bishop of London. He was berated bitterly for his lack of loyalty to Bishop Leo and the wider diocese.

Bryan then explained somewhat incautiously that Leo had his name forward for a different post and if he was successful he would be leaving the diocese. This might mean that Rev John could possibly survive in the Church of England but only because senior diocesan officials would have other matters to occupy their minds. He might remain a priest because he was too inconsequential for any new bishop to worry about. Nonetheless at the very least a stiffly worded report would be placed permanently on John's file for such a new bishop to read. Bryan then arrogantly indicated the meeting was over, got up and opened his office door.

Chapter 16
The Future Is Assured

The next few weeks into late summer witnessed frenzied activity around Abchurch Yard. Rev John found himself monitoring the modernisation of St Mary Abchurch and drawing up the formal faculty document necessary for the diocese to approve the electrical and redecoration work proposed. In the event, the faculty was agreed in time, and John was charged by the diocese with overall responsibility for the progress of the work. He had ownership of the keys to the main door monitoring those who came in and went out. Roderick now arranged to employ the various companies and workmen necessary for the renovation to be undertaken.

A cacophony of joiners, stone masons, painters, electricians, heating engineers and cleaning staff rapidly moved into the church and the front yard. To the passerby, Abchurch Yard suddenly appeared to be in a permanent state of confusion especially so to the American Friends of St Mary Abchurch who brought its many members over to London to see the hectic work being undertaken both inside and outside the church. These same American visitors could never be kept out of the actual building of course as they had funded much of the work so a passage was eventually configured on temporary wooden boards placed throughout the church for them to walk through safely to watch the activities of the workmen up close. City of London guides also added to the controlled pandemonium. Denied entry to the magnificent building for many months they now returned with significant numbers of domestic and international visitors.

That summer it seemed the whole world was talking about St Mary Abchurch. Everyone wanted to witness the renovation of Abchurch at first hand and all wanted to buy an association badge as if to prove to eternity that they were indeed there at the beginning of the story. Such was the interest that the workmen constantly complained, albeit quietly, that they could achieve quicker results if they were just left alone to do their work.

Nancy, Karen and Roderick decided early on that it would make sense to work to an end date in the new year to focus the minds of all, and so a day in the first week of March was chosen to complete the work. By early January, the building had been rewired and modern spotlights fixed into the dome, near the reredos and on some of the best wall monuments including that to Patience Ward. The organ was cleaned and renovated. The outside walls were washed thoroughly taking away the grime of centuries and the great clear glass windows were polished inside and out. Winter sunshine now made them sparkle.

One day whilst watching the workmen polish the wooden reredos and seeing that the modernised church was finally taking shape, Karen had started to think about who would be the minister, the vicar, in St Mary Abchurch, the incumbent who would follow Aubrey Braithwaite. She knew from experience that the wrong man or woman could be disastrous for all their plans. Bishop Leo had announced his elevation to the Province of York a few weeks before Christmas and as surprising as that announcement was it did at least mean that he and his acolytes would be separated from any appointment to St Mary Abchurch, and their dislike of Thomas Cranmer might quickly be forgotten.

Matters were soon resolved. Surprisingly, it was Aubrey himself who came forward with the solution. He had been quite taken with meeting the changed Rev John. And a friend who worked at St James Garlickhythe had reported to him that he had seen John praying in St James and reading the Book of Common Prayer. Aubrey wrote to Karen suggesting John might be the best choice.

Then, Bishop Leo's surprise elevation to York gave Rev John his chance to move into frontline ministry. He applied for the post of vicar of St Mary Abchurch and in the confusion of changes in the London diocese his appointment was quickly approved. So Aubrey had been right after all. His letter left with instructions for the next vicar of St Mary Abchurch had fortuitously indeed been picked up by that very person.

Karen and Nancy were delighted. "We couldn't be more pleased," said Nancy as she kissed John. "We know that our church will be in very safe hands."

"Save your approval until you have seen my first prayer book service," laughed John. "There really is an awful lot to learn and appreciate in that book, and I'm conscious I'm still a novice in all its ways."

"Don't fret, John," winked Karen. "We know the Church of England has picked the right man, and I know Rev Aubrey has approved. Remember you promised to go down to Suffolk to see him soon."

"Yes, of course," said John. "In fact, I was going to suggest our little team all went down one Sunday, so I can watch an old hand navigating Matins and Holy Communion through the Book of Common Prayer."

"Brilliant idea," laughed Nancy, "and we can all witness the 'And Finally' moment." The friends smiled.

Easter Sunday was chosen by the Abchurch Militant Association as the day when its members would officially show the world that the national and international campaign to save St Mary Abchurch had achieved success. Roderick's plans to relight, rewire, clean and paint the building inside and out were completed on time early that March. The wall monuments and the magnificent painted dome were now all illuminated anew. By the end of the month in excess of a staggering, five million people had signed the online petition. Roderick had visited several of the local businesses to explain that going forward St Mary Abchurch wanted to work closely with them.

The association had been mentioned in newspaper articles and television interviews across the globe. And, by now, the membership badge of the association, containing an image of the painted dome, could be seen everywhere, worn by old and young alike. Adverts on buses and trains showed the image stamped in one corner as many commercial companies from all over England wanted to be associated with what had been achieved. The plan therefore was that the association would say a warm thank you to these supporters and formerly close down its operations at Easter time, when they would be able proudly to show the world the new vibrant St Mary Abchurch.

And Easter Sunday indeed was truly a fitting day of Christian worship to celebrate success. Easter is after all the significant day of Christian rebirth, the most important occasion in the church's calendar, and, as many remarked, St Mary Abchurch had indeed itself been reborn. In a spirit of reconciliation, fitting for such a moment, at Nancy's suggestion, Bishop Leo, his wife Dorothy, Bryan, Jude and senior figures from TPL were invited to take part. Leo by then had been enthroned as the new Archbishop of York and both Jude and Bryan had followed him to the north of England.

No one replied from the diocese. The chairman of TPL alone accepted the invitation to attend matins, and he came with printed cards wishing the refreshed church a glorious future. Nancy and Karen welcomed him warmly. At the last moment, the association decided to advertise their achievement by inviting the world's media to witness the events.

Cameras, microphones and odd-shaped black boxes all joined by multicoloured wires were therefore put in place inside and outside the building on the evening before Easter Day itself. Roderick organised a flower festival of spring flowers and plants which added a wealth of happiness and colour to the day's proceedings. Numerous bunches of spring daffodils dotted around the church and bathed the whole building in warm yellow light.

The doors were flung open early for three spectacular services that day, early Holy Communion, 11:00 am Matins and at the end of it all a glorious choral Evensong. Someone remarked laughingly that the same people went to all three! And that was probably true. This Easter Sunday was such a warm and memorable day, helped by the bright spring sunshine, that clearly no one wanted to leave. All the pews were full including the ancient side ones which unusually faced into the body of the church; several extra benches dotted around Abchurch groaned with the weight of so many parishioners, and chairs were also crammed together to accommodate visitors in the small upstairs gallery. The packed church shone and sparkled as though it knew the world was watching.

Large painted images of Sir Christopher Wren were draped on all sides partly to say thank you to the great architect for designing St Mary Abchurch and partly to show that his building would never be allowed to die in the future. And all three services of course were heavily sprinkled with hymns from the old Anglican hymnal, Hymns Ancient and Modern. Television cameras recorded many of the day's events for the evening news. The church bell, which had been retuned only a few years before when Aubrey was the vicar, pealed out stridently over the City of London for many hours, operated by a rota of enthusiastic bell ringers. And the great bells of St Paul's seemed to answer in reply. The famous cathedral was obviously delighted that his Abchurch daughter had survived so well.

The morning celebration of matins became the principal service for many parishioners on that day. Aubrey and Joan had taken the train to London the day before and stayed overnight with Nancy. Aubrey had been asked to preach and read prayers that morning, and of course, he added the Easter Anthems set out in the prayer book before the Collect for that special occasion.

Once in the pulpit, he intoned, "Christ is risen from the dead: and become the first fruits of them that slept."

During his sermon, his white Salisbury surplice, lovingly washed, ironed and pressed by Joan, picked up the sunshine now streaming into the building from Abchurch Yard through the freshly cleaned sparkling windows. In his Suffolk church, it was a tradition for the incumbent to wear Geneva bands round the neck when preaching so today he had decided to bring the practice to St Mary Abchurch. However, it was Karen, planning for every eventuality, who had enacted a firm promise from him not to say 'and finally' at any point in his Easter sermon.

"I think one or two of us might burst out laughing if you did," she had explained winking.

Many from the Vintry, delighted to have played a big part in saving Abchurch, helped fill the pews, and the manager, having been secretly financed by Roderick, agreed to open the pub as an exception throughout that Sunday to ensure singing throats did not become too dry. He moreover insisted on telling everyone as often as possible, to Joan's embarrassment, that he had ordered two extra bottles of cream sherry for Mr and Mrs Vicar.

"He only says that to annoy me," Joan had laughed.

Rev John led all three services, still apologising for his lack of familiarity with Thomas Cranmer's Book of Common Prayer although, by now, he was reciting the chants and prayers as if weened on the prayer book. Bob played the organ to his usual very high standard throughout the day, although an observant communicant might have noticed that he did occasionally falter because the sheer joy, excitement and warmth of the occasion often brought tears to his eyes. In the afternoon, the Guildhall School of Music and Drama sent an orchestra of final-year students to augment Bob's organ music. And it was at their suggestion that some of Mahler's music was played. So it was that at Easter Evensong in the early evening the choir, performing together with organ and orchestra, sang with a special inner happiness crescendoing parts of Mahler's great Resurrection Symphony which seemed so appropriate to bring Easter Sunday to a fitting close.

Its cascading finale ricocheted around the building. The great painted dome of St Mary Abchurch had surely never witnessed anything like it since it was constructed centuries before during the time of Sir Christopher Wren. God's House was now reopened for all. And later at the suggestion of the new Bishop of London a marble plaque was fixed to the west wall which paid fulsome tribute to Karen, Nancy and Roderick for their dedication and perseverance.

Postscript

St Mary Abchurch had survived intact, its brilliantly apportioned and painted dome, instead of being cut up into pieces, continued to rest maternally, sensitively lit, over the whole edifice. The church's imaginative restoration and relighting quickly became a showpiece to inspire and educate architectural students from around the world. Over the next few years and well into the second half of the twenty-first century, guides would automatically include it on all of their tours. The City Corporation erected beautifully designed wooden signposts near the Mansion House and the Bank of England more easily to direct visitors to Abchurch Yard.

No visit to the City of London could be fully accomplished without a stop to see the now famous church with its magnificent painted dome, the Grinling Gibbons carvings, the covered font, the ancient poor boxes and the wooden pulpit. Overseas tourists in particular knew that if they mentioned the City of London to friends at home they would be asked if they had visited St Mary Abchurch. Such indeed would become its fame.

Its renovation was only part of the story of course. Some would claim but a subsidiary part. Many later historians, chronicling the unexpected re-awakening of Christianity in

England at this time, would acknowledge the part played in that great religious and cultural revival by the evangelical leadership provided unstintingly by the incumbents of St Mary Abchurch. They were helped of course by new senior leadership in the Anglican Communion. A series of inspirational bishops and archbishops, many of whom had preached at St Mary Abchurch, now led the Church of England, the best assortment of senior clerics since the Reformation it was said.

Future generations would often date this religious rebirth, coming as it did with a renewed understanding and appreciation of England's rich history, to the time of the noisy international campaign to save this building from demolition. Numerous churches abroad would now be twinned with St Mary Abchurch, and the Church of St Thomas on Fifth Avenue in New York City was even rumoured to be considering marking its association by unveiling a celebratory blue plaque in the London tradition.